THE
THREE LEGGED
TEA TABLE

THE
THREE LEGGED
TEA TABLE

SARADINDU

PARTRIDGE
A Penguin Random House Company

To order additional copies of this book, contact
Partridge India
000 800 10062 62
www.partridgepublishing.com/india
orders.india@partridgepublishing.com

Contents

ACKNOWLEDGEMENTS

Thanks to both my parents for all their support, especially to my father who is my role model, love you both. Thanks again to my father for all the corrections and editing the manuscript.

My sincere thanks to Mr. Niloy Sen for the cover design and all the illustrations.

A special thanks to Payel for her inspirations, suggestions, feedbacks and criticisms. My thanks also to her for all her help in digitizing the illustrations.

My extended thanks to Mr. Nelson Cortez, Ms. Ann Minoza and everyone at Partridge who helped me in making my dream come true.

THE THREE LEGGED TEA TABLE

03 . . . . 02 . . . . 01 . . . . 00 . . . . The light for the pedestrians turned green. A stream of human beings crossed one of the busiest streets of the city. Most of them were holding umbrellas over their heads or wearing raincoats. This was the last week of October, but since yesterday there has been a low pressure area formation over the Bay of Bengal which resulted in heavy to very heavy rainfall in the past twenty-four hours. Kolkata looked damp and shabby; there was also news of water logging in few parts of the city especially in the low areas. Deepak was among one of the people who were just crossing Park Street, his destination was the popular tea bar just opposite of the road. He was wearing black half sleeved T-shirt, a pair of light blue jeans with a pair of kito sandals.

That day was Saturday, half day at the office. Deepak entered the tea bar, closed his umbrella and sat at his favourite table beside the big glass window in their favourite tea bar. He normally ordered black tea, but looking at the damp weather outside he ordered a cup of lemon tea. It was served to him within a few minutes. Due to this weather, the tea bar was comparatively less crowded. While sipping the lemon tea and relishing the untimely rain outside, Deepak was waiting for his two best friends to arrive. Together these three never missed their chance to meet once a week, on Saturdays. These weekly meetings by now have become a tradition and essential part of their life. None of their week was complete without these weekly meetings, and if by any chance any one of them missed it, that week turned out to be a miserable and long for them till their next meet.

Deepak checked the digital clock of his mobile; it's only ten minutes past four. As his office was on Park Street itself, he was always the first one to arrive. Subhashis, who worked in a multinational company based at Theatre Road not very far from here, was normally the second to arrive. While their third friend Anuraddha, who worked at the Kolkata branch of a reputed US based creative agency, based at Ballygunge was the last one to arrive.

Those three have been friends since childhood; it's been more than two decades since they knew each other. Three of them read in the same co-educational convent school. From school to college, from college to university and from university to their respective fields, they might have changed their respective fields but their friendship did not diminish. Their inseparable friendship was envious to many. While Deepak was on the midway of his lemon tea, he found Subhashis approaching the tea bar. An automatic smile came to Deepak's face. He was wearing a light coloured formal shirt and black trousers with a threefold black umbrella to protect him from the rain.

"Welcome! Welcome! How are you?" enquired Deepak. Subhashis smiled back and put back his umbrella inside a plastic carry bag. He then pulled a chair and took a seat beside Deepak. His tie was peeping from his breast pocket. A single chair was now laid vacant for their third friend.

"I am fine, Deep. Thank you. How are you?" Subhashis greeted him back.

"I am also ok. Well as good as you can be in this washed out weather." Deepak replied.

Both of them laughed.

Subhashis then ordered his regular cup of masala tea. The two friends started conversing and updating each other. After a while Subhashis said; "Where is Anu? She is coming today, right?"

"Of course Subha; before I came here I called on her cell. She told me that due to this weather there are less buses plying on the road. She will be here any time soon."

While they were talking this they saw a familiar figure crossing their window and entered the tea bar. The figure was wearing a nice floral pink coloured raincoat. It was Anuraddha. She opened and hanged the rain coat on a coat hanger beside the door and came towards her two waiting friends. She was wearing a body-hugging yellow T-Shirt and a pair of white flood pants. Her outfit nicely matched her perfect hourglass figure.

She came towards them and greeted them. "Hello Guys! It's really horrible to get transportation on a rainy weather. I had to wait for quite a while before I get a bus." She takes the only available chair and sat.

"Ooh!! I am feeling hungry. Did you guys order something?"

Both Deepak and Subhashis nodded their head; "But we two are also very hungry" added Subhashis.

Anuraddha ordered Chicken Spiral Pasta, Chicken Steak and Black Forest Pudding.

"So Anu, how is the office going?" Deepak asked.

"It's fine, the only problem was that no matter how much pressure we put the deadline always catches us before we finish. And my boss Supriya Madam, these days she is on the edge of her nerves. Well I can't blame her, these days headquarter sent one of their representatives named Julie, Julie Francis Andrews, to oversee the operation of their branch office and my boss hardly misses any chance to impress her. And her favourite show-off is shouting at us." Both Deepak and Subhashis laughed "Though Julie is a gem of a lady; she has so many stories to tell. Frequently she takes our team to lunch and then she really opens up and shares her experiences."

"What about you guys?" she asked back.

"Well, for me there have not been many ups and downs at office. As you all know my workplace is quite uneventful and boring. All my workmates are also quite boring. They prefer to come to the office on time, complete their work and leave after completing. We don't have any bossy boss like Anu's or any colourful characters like Subha's colleagues. I am really deprived of these spices at office front. Sometimes I really feel like running from this office. It's really boring at times." Deepak paused "But recently something really interesting happened in my aunt's family. I am sure you two remember Shila aunty, whose husband is a famous doctor and her son, is an engineer studying in USA and her daughter is a doctor, who against everyone's wish went to the rural village to practice."

Both Subhashis and Anuraddha said that they did very well remember.

"Well, she returned last week. I went to my aunt's house to give Ruku di a visit. She had a long story to tell."

"What about you Subha?" Deepak asked.

The waiter came and placed their orders. For the next few minutes all of them kept on concentrating on the food. All of them seemed quite hungry. After they finished their pasta, steak followed by the pudding, they ordered two cups of tea and a cup of cappuccino. Anuraddha went to use the washroom. On returning with a fresh coat of lipstick, she found their respective beverages already served.

"So Subha, tell us how is your multinational running?" Anuraddha sometimes teased Subhashis by sarcastically terming his office as multinational. It was true that it indeed was a reputed multinational but she used to tease him due it its strict business etiquette and strict dress code. They are not even allowed casual on weekends and even suspended few employees for breaking the rule. Anuraddha even teased him by saying him to go to bed by wearing formal dress and tie or else he would be suspended if his superior found him not properly dressed when they would come in his dream.

Subhashis said "This week in office was different. Previous week, while at office, suddenly my senior Sudip da received a call and left in a hurry, he didn't answer to anyone then. This week, after he joined, he broke a story to us. We came to know he suddenly had to go to North Bengal. All of us who were present there were completely awestruck by what we heard. It was something we all didn't expect. He told us the story of his friend, another senior at the office named Amit da. Though I personally did not work with him or know much about him, I only knew him by his face though I knew that both Sudip and Amit were really close friends. The rest of the week, the story becomes our major point of discussion. Everywhere, in the cafeteria or in the men's room, someone or the other were discussing about it."

"What is the story?" both Deepak and Anuraddha asked curiously at the same time. "This weather is perfect for stories as we couldn't go outside, though I thought to visit the nearby mall, but this weather killed my mood to step outside. So let us hear the story. Listening to stories is really great way to pass your time." Anuraddha added.

Subhashis picked his cup and took a large sip. He put the cup down and began . . . .

RAT-TAT-TAT

When Amit came into the bungalow, it was raining heavily.

Amit heard about this old British bungalow from his colleague, Sudip. Sudip visited this part of North Bengal a couple of years ago with his family and quite accidentally, he saw that bungalow. Their jeep, while going from Kurseong to Darjeeling had a flat tire at a place near this bungalow. This wooden bungalow in a quiet place looked to have perfectly fitted on the lap of the nature. The place looked very calm and quiet with nice flora and fauna around it. A name of some British officer's was inscribed on the door, which Sudip could not recall, while narrating the story to Amit. Sudip could view the nice and perfect vision of the mighty Kanchenjunga from that spot. He imagined that the occupants were so lucky that they used to get the nice view daily from their bedroom windows.

But the bungalow seemed quite uninhabited to Sudip.

In the meantime, their driver came and told him that the jeep was ready. He asked the driver about the bungalow. The driver told him not to go to those unknown places alone. Long time ago, this place belonged to some army officer, but now a day, nobody lived there.

What a waste of a nice property! Easily, this place could be utilized in a more meaningful way, he thought while going towards Darjeeling. That place, now, became just a memory for him.

When Amit told him that he was planning to visit some quiet place near Darjeeling or Sikkim, Sudip immediately told him about the bungalow. He also told Amit that he did not know the procedure how to get that bungalow.

Amit told Sudip to provide him with the necessary information and the rest he could manage.

Both Amit and Sudip worked in a multinational company in Kolkata. Their office was located on Theatre Road. Both of them crossed their mid-thirties; Sudip was a few years older than Amit. Sudip was married, had a son of five years, and named Bubun. Amit was unmarried he lived at Ballygunge in his own flat. Sunita, Sudip's wife, continuously teased him to get married. She even proposed a few matches for him, which Amit smartly rejected with a smile. Amit stayed alone in this city. He never said a word about his parents and his friends never asked him about his family.

Sudip, Sunita and Bubun became very close to him and Bubun called him uncle.

Amit was planning to visit North Bengal for quite a long time. He wanted to stay in a calm and quiet place, away from the crowd. He was looking for a place, might be a cottage or bungalow, where he could stay alone, only with himself. He wanted to stay with nature at least for a few days.

Amit told Sudip about his desire in the office, Sudip then described him about that bungalow. Though Sudip could not provide him with many details, he called up one of his school friends, named Nirmal.

Nirmal ran a travel agency near Esplanade. He invited Amit a couple of days after and told him that there was a bungalow matching his description. But that bungalow was uninhabited for a long, long time.

Nirmal told him that the bungalow was, at one time, belonged to Col. William Mackenzie, a notorious army officer in the British era. After taking retirement from the armed forces, he took up the post of Manager in some Tea estate. His ruthless nature continued there. But there was a mishap at that place. Nirmal could not tell him what really happened to Col. Mackenzie, but that place, from that time, was uninhabited. Only a caretaker looked after the bungalow.

Nirmal also told Amit that he could arrange for permission to stay in that place within a few days, from his contacts with the Tea board. Amit readily agreed.

Within two weeks, Amit applied for leave from his office. As Amit did not take any leave for last one year, his boss, Mr. Bakshi did not bother to sanction his leave. He only raised his eyebrow, when he heard about the plan of Amit's holidays.

When Sunita heard about his plan, she sternly objected and said that there were so many options to stay in and around Darjeeling. Why was he planning to stay all alone in an unknown place, at the mercy of a local caretaker who could take any advantage on him?

As usual, Amit gave her a nice smile and smartly declined her objection.

Amit himself was very excited about his trip. He always wanted to stay in the lap of the Himalayas all by himself. There should not be anyone between the nature and himself. And, this season between autumn and winter, the nature would be fresh, green and bright after months of monsoon. As per the description, this bungalow would perfectly suit his needs.

"Why this bungalow remained uninhabited for a long time? So many things could be done with this place. It could be turned into a hotel, resort or anything," Amit thought.

Anyway, Amit was very happy that he got the place of his choice. He thanked his luck and thanked Sudip for giving him information about this place. He started daydreaming about the beauty of the bungalow.

On the 13th of October, he set out for his trip. He had booked a Tata Sumo for the whole trip. When he was approaching Raiganj, he found the weather started worsening.

"It could be a depression" thought Amit.

Though he did not care about a bad weather, his only concern was any landslide in the hilly area.

When he crossed Siliguri and took the road to Darjeeling, it was already 6.30A.M. He thought to take a break. His driver Chhotelal also needed a good rest. He found an empty roadside stall and asked Chhotelal to park the Sumo near it. The driver was very happy to get the break. He was driving continuously after their dinner at Krishnanagar. They only stopped at Malda for a tea break. Rain was lightened for a while but Amit was sure that the rain would bounce back at any moment.

Probably due to bad weather, there was less traffic on the road.

"It would be better if we could reach the spot before further worsening the weather." thought Amit.

This eatery was managed by a middle aged Tibetan, might be his family lived at the backside of the eatery"

Amit ordered a plate of Momo with hot soup. Chhotelal ordered a bowl of thupka. He sat at a distance and started eating, the moment it was served.

Amit started looking around started gulping the nature through his eyes. He filled his lungs with fresh air.

"Oh! This oxygen is so pure, so fresh!"

He found, the manager was smiling and waiting for him. Those Tibetans, who were mostly refugees, are very friendly. Their hearts are very pure and simple. Amit smiled back and came to sit on the bench, the manager sat opposite to him.

"Where are you heading, Sahib? Darjeeling or Sikkim?" asked the Tibetan in Hindi.

"None of these places", Amit replied with a smile.

"Then, Sahib?"

Amit describe his destination. Suddenly the smile of the manager vanished. His small eyes widened.

"Ma—Ma-Mackenzie Bungalow? Why, Sahib?" The Tibetan pleaded, "Please don't go to that place."

"Why? What is the wrong with that place? I had heard that it is a nice spot. There is an excellent view of the Kanchenjunga from that bungalow. I had planned and arranged for this trip for quite a long time. Why should I not go there?" asked Amit.

"That place is not good, Sahib. The ghost of bad Mackenzie sahib still visits that place every night"

"What nonsense!" laughed Amit.

"No Sahib, it is not nonsense. Every one of this place knows about that bungalow, but none of us dare to visit that bungalow even during the daytime. You can ask anyone. Why do you think that the place has been lying vacant for so long time? The Tea Company occupied that place, but they also sent no one there."

"But the bungalow has a caretaker. If there is a ghost, do you think he could be there for a long time?" asked Amit.

Entering through the huge gate, Amit saw the name, "MACKENZI BUNGLOW" inscribed on a white marble slab.

"Tamang is the servant of his ghost master. He prays for his master. Tamang is an evil, we don't talk to him and he also doesn't mix with anyone. Whenever he comes to the market, he hardly speaks to anybody. He points to the things, which he wants to buy, and the shopkeeper gives him immediately and let him go from his shop as soon as possible. Everyone avoids him.

"Gurung is the gardener of that place. Even he doesn't stay there at night. Gurung also avoids Tamang. Gurung heard Tamang to speak with his master for many times." The manager told Amit in one breath.

"But this is not possible. Ghosts are fictitious and I don't believe in ghosts." Amit replied.

"You city people do not believe in ghosts. But those spirits are very much alive in these places. Possibly you don't know the story of that bad white Sahib." The manager told again.

"What is the story?" asked Amit.

"Hmmm! Long, long ago, I heard this story from the local people of the hill and they also in turn, had heard from their forefathers," said the manager.

"The British were then the ruler of this country. There was an army officer, named William Mackenzie. He was very aggressive and hardworking He was very ruthless also. He hated the natives to the core of his heart. Mainly due to his image and aggression, he gradually promoted to the rank of a colonel much quicker than expected.

"It was heard that he nearly killed his syce only by whipping. As he could not hold his horse stand still while he was mounting his horse. He later shot the horse for its rudeness. Once few local boys, at a lazy afternoon, trespassed his garden to get some juicy mangoes.

Mackenzie's siesta was disturbed by them. His servants caught all of them. Mackenzie crushed their fingers under his boots. All the four kids could not use their right hands for the rest of their lives.

"So ruthless and ill-tempered he was in his nature, that everybody feared him, even his seniors."

The manager continued his story, "When the first great war broke (World War 1), Col. Mackenzie was sent to Africa to serve the Royal Army. There were many stories about his aggression and ruthlessness.

"After more than one year staying in Africa, he returned to India. People found him using a stick and were found limping a bit. It was heard that at one night, while fighting, he was hit by a bullet on his left knee. He fell into a trench and stayed there for two days without food and water. When his force found him, he was down with fever. They brought him to the medical camp, but it was too late. Though, after a long treatment, his wound healed but it damaged his left leg and was left to limp for the rest of his life

"The local people thought that the ill-tempered Mackenzie got his due from the Almighty, and would repent for his evil deeds for the rest of his life. But they were all wrong. The bullet had just left a mark on his body, but it could not touch his soul. His beastly nature remained the same, if not more. He became more ruthless and violent than before. He one day shoot his barber, when he accidently cut the cheek of his master while shaving. Before killing the barber, Mackenzie made deep cut marks all over the barber's face with his own knife. The face could not be recognized. Whoever saw that bruised face, took them a long time to forget.

"Mackenzie resigned from the army and took a post of a manager of a Tea Estate near this place with the help of his friend, named Drake."

The manager stopped for some time to recall his memory. He started again to go into details, "The people of this place could hardly imagine what terror was waiting for them. Mackenzie bought a bungalow and named it under his name. That wooden bungalow had a nice panoramic view of the Kanchenjunga. It was situated at the end of a cliff, which went several feet and vanished in the dense forest below. Within a few days, the people of this part of the valley and mainly the Tea Estate, where he joined as manager, came to know about the nature and temper of the terror, named Mackenzie."

"You could hardly find a butt at that time which did not get a kick of his boot. It was heard when he arrived there was a labour problem in the Tea Estate. The locals were led by some left-influenced Bengali Babus, they had planned to go on a strike only to show the manager that they were backed by some organization and they could place their demands to the authority in the future. Pity for them that they did not know, they were dealing with perhaps the most ruthless and inhumane British officer in their life. One fine morning, when they gathered at the gate of the main office building, Mackenzie came on his horse and put a lasso around the neck of their leader. He dragged him throughout the village, most probably through the whole Estate, so that everyone could witness their leader's fate. Mackenzie finally arrived at the market area with the victim, who was half dead by then, clothes torn into pieces. Mackenzie puts his rope around his neck and hanged him on a tree. When the leader was dead, Mackenzie put five bullets in his body and one on his head, which burst like a pumpkin. The people of that area were so shocked and terrified that they dared to put the body of their leader down for two days. No one knew who put his body down. That tree still exists in the market." The Tibetan manager closed his eyes and remained silent for a few moments.

Amit was shocked by the narration." My God! What a cruel and a beastly man he was!" Amit resisted his emotion and asked the manager, "What happened next?"

Amit saw that his driver was out of the eatery and smoking a cigarette. He was surely becoming impatient, Amit thought. Rain could begin at any moment. But Amit did not want to miss the end part of the story.

The manager continued, "Mackenzie found a new toy to play with."

"And the toys were local women. Frequently he used to take young or middle aged women forcibly from his Tea Estate. Those women came back to the village the next day, bruised and mark of burnt cigar on their bodies. Everyone could make out what happened to them but none to speak a word about those mishaps. What the tortures they had gone through! Few of them committed suicide but most of them continued their lives, as they had no other option. Their husbands or members of their families remained silent for the fear that they might face the same fate like that Bengali leader or even worse."

"There was a girl named Lachhmi in the village at that time, crossed her eighteen years. Her parents locked her inside the house most of the time for fear of the lust of Mackenzie. It was heard that she was very pretty. She had a secret relationship with a local doctor, named Bhusan. He was also afraid of that lascivious Mackenzie.

Mackenzie himself had never shown any cruelty to Bhusan, probably because; he was a doctor, and the only doctor within miles.

"No one knew how Mackenzie got the information about Lachhmi, but he appeared to their house in one evening, he got down from his horse with a little difficulty. His damaged leg always used to give him some trouble at the time getting down or riding the horse. He broke into Lachhmi's house and forcefully took Lachhmi with him. Her father looked stunned and overwhelmed; he knew that he had no power to save his daughter. Lachhmi's mother fell on the feet of Mackenzie, begged, and cried. She even offered herself to Mackenzie and pleaded to spare her daughter. But all appeal fell to deaf ear."

"No one knew what happened on that night. Everyone was expecting the return of bruised and tortured Lachhmi to return, but she did not come back. When it was past afternoon, everybody was worried for Lachhmi. Did she, like others, commit suicide to get rid of ashamed life?

The next morning, a servant from the bungalow came to Lachhmi's house and told her father that his Sahib wanted to meet him. When he asked what happened to Lachhmi, to every one's surprise, the servant replied that she was alright. Lachhmi's father rushed to the bungalow of Mackenzie, a few villagers accompanied him. No one stopped them or asked any question. When they came inside the big hall, they were asked to sit. They looked around the nicely decorated huge wooden hall of the bungalow."

The manager continued his narration, "They heard a thundering voice, "Please be seated." The villagers were taken aback hearing that thunder-like voice. Everyone jumped on their toes and turned around.

"Please take your seat" Mackenzie told in broken Hindi. They were surprised to see a smile on his face. A rare sight perhaps a native had ever seen. But that was their beginning of their surprises.

"Who is Lachhmi's father?" asked Mackenzie.

Lachhmi's father came trembling in front of Mackenzie. But the next thing what he heard was perhaps most shocking in his life. It was strange to all that he survived the shock.

"Look sir, I want to marry your daughter. Please accept this proposal."

Everybody present there could not believe their ears. They thought what kind of joke it was. Was it a new game of Mackenzie? Everyone started looking at each other's face."

"Bapu!"

All of them turned around and found that Lachhmi came from inside the bungalow. Their eyes became wide at once when they found that Lachhmi was untouched as before. There was not even a single scratch on her or not a sign of torture. She looked fresher than before.

"Bapu!' Lachhmi again called her father. "Accept his proposal. You cannot resist him, if he wants to take me forcibly. But he is giving you a proposal of marriage and seeking your permission. Please believe me, I am all right. I am not ill-treated and I am still your daughter, Lachhmi. I am untouched and chaste. Believe me; this is for the benefit and wellness of all."

Lachhmi's father folded his hands, touched his forehead and bowed to Mackenzie.

Lachhmi ran towards her father and embraced him. Both of them started crying.

Mackenzie turned around and left the hall.

No one knew till date what really happened that night.

William Mackenzie married to Lachhmi two days later in a local church. Since then, Lachhmi was known as Anna Mackenzie.

Everyone realized that Mackenzie was a changed man. He was no longer cruel or inhumane. There was no news of his torture heard from then onwards."

"So this is how the story ended!" Amit told with a smile.

"No Sahib, if this story could end in this manner, it would not bother the local people till date after so many years." The manager continued, "I would be requesting you not to go there.

"Destiny had already written some different ending. Lachhmi, sorry, Anna and Mackenzie's married life passed one year. The changed Mackenzie looked after the Tea Estate, concentrated on his job, returned to his bungalow for lunch and his siesta. Again went to the Estate for a few hours and came back to the bungalow, where Anna used to wait for him. Mackenzie loved Anna a lot. The people of the locality breathed a sigh of great relief and they came out of the terror of Mackenzie.

"But the servants of the bungalow knew a different story. Every day, when Mackenzie went out to visit the Tea Estate, Doctor Bhusan came to the bungalow. At the beginning, the servants were informed that Anna had some secret disease, so she needed to be checked up regularly. But gradually, the matter was cleared to all of them. Their long hours of talking, giggles, laughing narrated a different story. Day by day, the time for private checking increased, now a day, nearly an hour or more.

"The secret love between Lachhmi and Doctor Bhusan was no longer a secret to the servants of the bungalow."

"The servants of Mackenzie loved Anna a lot. They realized that Anna knew a magic, as she had changed their cruel master completely. The presence of their master did not terrify them now. They did not want their master to go back to his former state of mood. So they healed the secret affair of Anna and did not disclose anything to their master.

"But secret things can never be a secret forever, one day it comes out to broad daylight. So was the case of Anna and Doctor Bhusan. Nobody knew how Mackenzie was informed about the affair."

"That day, it was raining heavily. Suddenly, Mackenzie was found rushing out of his office dashing a clerk, who was coming to him with a file. He pushed the clerk so heard that the head of the clerk banged on the wall. Mackenzie rode his horse and rushed towards his bungalow. While going very fast, he injured some people who came in his way, but Mackenzie did not slow down his horse."

"What exactly happened at that time, no one could tell. But there were some versions of the ending. Some locals concluded that Mackenzie's servants got the news of coming of Mackenzie and they arranged Anna and Doctor Bhusan to flee from the bungalow and to hide in the deep forest. Some of the villagers had their assumption that Mackenzie reached the bungalow just in time and killed Anna and Bhusan and threw them down the cliff."

Nobody ever saw Anna and Bhusan and did not even hear of them.

Mackenzie was found dead the next morning. He had shot himself with his revolver.

A prescription was found near his dead body which confirmed that Anna was pregnant."

"From that night onwards, it was said that Col. Mackenzie appeared in his bungalow, might be in search for his dear Anna. Or, he came there to take revenge. Whatever would be the reason, Mackenzie's ghost still haunts the bungalow.

"After that mishap, all the servants fled away one by one. Many officers of the Estate tried to stay in that bungalow, but all of them gave up their desire. Those who wanted to stay there at their own will faced fatal death. Gradually the bungalow became a haunted house. The Tea Company deputed a caretaker and a gardener to look after the bungalow. Only Tamang stayed there for a long time. He might have been staying there for about fifty years or more. His father was also the caretaker of that bungalow." The manager stopped for a while, then said in a friendly tone, "Please Sahib, don't go there. There are so many places in and around Darjeeling. Why to go to that cursed place? One of my relatives runs a hotel in Darjeeling; I can arrange everything, if you wish. It is very near to Mall."

"Well, well, well! The story of Col. Mackenzie is very interesting. I had never heard anything like this before. By the way how you have come to know the story in such a detail?"

The people of this place could hardly imagine what terror was waiting for them.

"Every local of this area knows the story in details, Sahib."

"Very well, then, let me tell you once again." Amit replied. "I had a dream to stay in that bungalow for a quite long time and I had taken all necessary measures and permission from the authority. Besides, I am not going to disturb the ghost of Col. Mackenzie. With due respect to him, he can share a space with me in that bungalow for just a few days.

"Don't worry, mister, I will be all right there. After returning, I shall again share a plate of momo in your stall."

Unwillingly, the manager gave him the details of the road that would lead them to the bungalow of Mackenzie. The place was not far from there. When the driver of Amit started the Sumo, it started raining.

"Sir, what was that manager telling you for such a long time," Chhotelal asked Amit.

"It was a nice story about that place." Amit replied. He did not disclose the story to his driver, as Chhotelal was also a villager and had various types of superstitions. The story he heard from the manager was touched and shocked him. He was analysing the story on his way.

"Sir, don't believe or mix with those refugees. Nearly all of them are drug peddlers and smugglers." Chhotelal told Amit while driving.

"Hmmm!" Sounded Amit, though he was deeply thinking about the story, he had just heard.

By following the direction of the manager, they reached the bungalow within fifteen minutes.

The moment Amit saw the bungalow, his heart filled with joy. Really the bungalow looked very nice from outside. If the weather became clear, he was sure, the gloomy grey background would be filled with nice picturesque of Kanchenjunga.

When the Sumo entered the premises, torrential rain began.

Entering through the huge gate, Amit saw the name, "MACKENZI BUNGLOW" inscribed on a white marble slab in the stylish bold block letters. This type of font, he had seen in many a British era buildings in Kolkata. Chhotelal brought the Sumo near the main entrance. He started blowing horn. Amit saw a figure coming out from the house. When the figure was visible, he thought him to be an old Nepali or a Bhutanese.

"This could be the caretaker, Tamang," thought Amit.

Amit remembered immediately that the manager told him, "Tamang was associated with his ghost master, Mackenzie. He was an evil." But this was an old and fragile man. If this man was found evil, had no chance to do any harm to a young and well-built man like Amit.

Tamang's face was heavily wrinkled due to his age. Looking at his face, his age would not be made out. It could be anything from sixty to eighty.

Looking at the face of that man, Amit suddenly remembered the fate of Mackenzie's barber, as told by the manager.

Amit introduced himself to the man, "Hi! I am Amit, I took permission . . ." He suddenly stopped. Tamang without showing any expression, took his suitcase, which Chhotelal carried from the back of Sumo, and started walking towards the inside the bungalow.

"What a strange man!" thought Amit.

"Hey, wait." Amit rushed behind the caretaker.

Tamang stopped near a room and went inside. Then the caretaker said, "You should not mess your room. Lunch will be served at 1PM and dinner at 8PM. No personal orders and no room service. This is not a hotel."

"Electricity was down since last night, no idea when it will resume. I shall provide you with a lantern." Tamang said all in one breathe in Hindi.

Amit was quite surprised by the behaviour of Tamang. He promised himself not to mingle much with that old freak. He had come here to enjoy the nature and he should have it.

Tamang said, "The Tea Company Babu came yesterday and told me that you are coming and instructed me to take good care of you. I replied to them that I shall do everything as far as my strength will permit. Seeing the weather, I thought that you are not coming. I don't know why you people do come over here. You people spread stories about this bungalow. I shall now arrange for your lunch." The old man turned back to leave the room. At the time of leaving, he said, "Don't throw lighted matchsticks or burnt cigarette ends on the floor. Remember, this is a wooden bungalow."

Amit stood still for a few moments. What kind of person was this Tamang? The manager told him that Tamang was an evil. But Amit found no evilness in him. He might be a bit psychic or might be the longer stay all alone in a forlorn house brought him in such state. He might not have learned or had forgotten how to talk normally. There could be months or years, he hardly talked to anyone. Anyway, Amit wiped out the episode of Tamang from his mind and surveyed the place, where he wanted to stay for a few days.

He started looking all around. It was indeed a nice bungalow, mostly made of wood. This place was yet to have colonial aggression. His room might have used as a living room in the past. It had a fireplace, a few chairs and a wooden sofa with a centre table in front of it. The room had minimal furniture, but very neatly kept. A long wooden pole was dangling from the ceiling, which ran across the breadth of the room. Amit thought, why this pole was there and what its use was. Then he remembered that the use of hand pulled fan of that era. He came to the balcony and found a rope was attached to the pole. No curtain was hanging from that pole. But he could imagine of that time when this room was used that a native used to pull the rope continuously to provide air to the occupant of the room to give him cool comfort in the summer. He found there were a few chairs on the balcony. Amit observed from the balcony that a man, wearing a raincoat, attending the plants of the garden. "This could be Gurung, the gardener," thought Amit. He could meet him later.

He came inside and started exploring the other parts of the bungalow. He spent the rest of the morning doing it. In his room, he found a single cot, which was unusual for a living of a British. He came to the conclusion that it might have shifted from some other room. Most of the rooms were closed, a few of them which remained unlocked, were dumped with old furniture. Those rooms were not so tidy and bore a mark that those rooms were taken less care.

In the main hall area, Amit saw a huge fireplace, three large sofa sets, many decorated furniture. Few of them stuffed animal heads including a tiger, two leopards and a rhino. This hall was decorated with many rifles and revolvers. Looking at the arms, Amit thought that many of these arms had tasted blood of many natives including that left—influenced Bengali leader. A whip and a hunter were also pinned on the wall. He turned around and shocked in awe. A huge oil painting of an army officer was staring at him. His cruel eyes were burning, as it seemed to Amit. He unknowingly retarded two steps.

This man in the oil painting was really cruel. Thick golden eyebrows, large moustache, long love-lock covering his cheeks really made him ferocious to look at.

He thanked God that the owner of those eyes had died long ago and Amit was fortunate to look at his oil painting.

He came back to his room. He again started analysing the whole story in his mind. He could not remember how much time had passed but the words of the Tibetan manager flashed back into his mind, "Every night, Mackenzie's ghost comes back to his bungalow."

Amit also saw a black and white photograph of a local girl, wearing a Western gown in one of the unlocked rooms. That photograph was in tittering condition, but Amit could easily recognize the person. Surely, it was the photograph of Lachhmi alias Anna, whom Mackenzie loved a lot and whose presence changed the life of the ruthless Colonel. The rain had stopped for a while, but could be started at any moment. Amit, after freshening himself, had his lunch. Tamang was not a bad cook. He arranged rice, egg, curry and simple vegetables. In such a bad weather, this lunch seemed heaven to him. After his lunch, he stepped into the garden to get a full view of the bungalow. This bungalow was in a beautiful location and acquired a huge space. The back yard was situated at the edge of the cliff and after that there were miles and miles of unobstructed view, which, on a clear day, would provide a panoramic sight of the Himalayas, especially of the Kanchenjunga. The surrounding garden was well maintained, 'Gurung had done a sincere job.' thought Amit. Though the bungalow was still livable, some portion of the house had been showing the marks of its age. Few planks were loose, some wooden railings were broken. Even he found a few broken windows at the back of the bungalow.

Overall it showed that the bungalow had remained uninhabited for a long time.

Amit planned to go near the cliff to see what was at the bottom of the cliff.

"Don't go there, Sahib." Amit heard a voice.

He turned around and found a man with a garden tool and a sapling in his hand. He said again, "Don't go there, please. It was several feet deep and the rain had loosened the soil. You could easily slip from there."

Amit failed to put his words aside and stepped back. He could easily recognize the gardener, named Gurung. He exchanged some words with the gardener. He began to like that person.

While he was planning to go inside, Gurung told him not to mix much with Tamang. That old fellow was not reliable at all. Gurung also advised him to close the door of his room tightly at night and not to open the door or to respond to any call. When Amit asked him the reason, he only told him to keep his words in mind. He could not tell him anymore. Amit himself would understand the matter.

Amit came inside and found that Chhotelal was waiting for him. He remembered that Chhotelal told him that he would go to visit his brother-in-law in Darjeeling, who ran a guest house there. He would come back by the next morning.

Soon after Chhotelal had left, Amit opened his suitcase and took out a Jeffery Archer's novel. He had brought some books with him planning to complete them during this vacation. He heard the footsteps of his driver and later the sound of Sumo was fading out. Then he was all alone. Lazily the afternoon had passed and the evening appeared.

Tamang had given him a big lantern in his room. This time Tamang placed the lantern down and left. He did not utter a word to Amit. Though the gloominess outside provided with some light, it was becoming darker by every passing moment. Amit tried to read in the light of the lantern, but his electricity-suited eyes did not allow him to read a few lines of the book. He closed the book and came to the balcony. It was dark all over. It seemed to him there was no sign of life anywhere. A few minutes ago, he could hear the snarl of a dog or howl of a fox, but now everything was covered with deep silence. He was feeling cold on the outside, so he entered the room and closed the door, which was closed with a creaking sound.

Falling ill in this lonely place was not desirable to him. He lay down on the bed and started thinking about the whole Mackenzie story. By looking on his oil painting was a shivering fact. What would be if that ruthless ghost was a real thing and what would be if that Mackenzie planned to visit the new occupant of his bungalow!

He turned around and shocked in awe. A huge oil painting of an army officer was staring at him.

Though Amit was not a superstitious man, but at that calm, quiet, silent and dark place some small amount of fear was developing in the mind of Amit, remembering the story of Mackenzie, narrated by the Tibetan manager. He could not feel how much time had passed, but suddenly he was alarmed by the footsteps of somebody approaching towards his room.

RAT TAT TAT

Amit was shocked and jumped to his feet, "Who is it, who is it?" shouted Amit.

"Dinner is ready," replied Tamang from outside.

Amit released a deep breath.

"Phew!"

It was Tamang. What a fool he was! Forgetting his dinner, he was afraid of a ghost in this century! He laughed at himself and opened the door. When there was silence prevailed all around, a negligible sound could make a person to shiver from the core of his heart. The footsteps of Tamang felt magnified several times. As he was thinking about the cruelness of Mackenzie, he had completely forgotten about anything.

He went with Tamang for dinner. This time, Tamang arranged roti and a preparation of egg. He said, "If the weather is not clear, tomorrow also you have to be satisfied with eggs. Supply of raw food is scanty. I, myself can eat anything, but you are the guest, you need to be treated properly. I can't let you have the same food every day."

Amit stopped chewing and looked at Tamang. This old man was not bad or evil at all, thought Amit. Then why everyone thought so about him! Amit told himself that he should interact with Tamang more to know him closely. Amit promised himself that he should try to start conversation with this man in the next day. Possibly, he knew the entire story in the details. When Amit was nearly finishing his dinner, a loud thunder struck nearby.

Tamang cursed, and told that the night weather would be going worse. He said, "Let's pray that there would not be a landslide or then every supply would be cut off. The storm seemed to be coming."

Amit finished his dinner and went towards his room. While he was passing the main hall, his eyes automatically fell on the oil painting of Mackenzie.

At that moment, there was a bright lightning of a thunder. Before blinding him for a few moments, it seemed to Amit that the picture of Mackenzie was laughing cruelly at him. His eyes looked fiercer than ever in the dazzling light. Amit could not risk a moment and hurriedly ran the last few yards to enter his room. He closed the door and found himself panting to breathe. He could not forget those awesome eyes. He could feel someone's presence in the hall. He smelt cigar. Amit found himself trembling. He could not believe in himself. Did he see it correctly or it was his imagination? What he was thinking, was not possible.

His reasonableness was slowly crumbling down. His educated mind was telling him not to believe in these things, but from his innermost core of his heart, he failed to keep them aside. He began to believe why this place was uninhabited for long years. He even planned to move in some safe hotel in the next morning. The storm started in its full strength. Every now and then, there was a deafening sound of thunder. The wind was blowing heavily banging the doors and windows. "Will this bungalow be able to survive this stormy night!" thought Amit.

Amit thought it would be foolish to stay awake. He dimmed the light and went inside the blanket. He put up a pillow over his head to restrict the sound to reach his ears. The storm of the hills is quite different from the plains, realized Amit. It seemed to him at every gash of the wind, the bungalow would be blown away.

Amit could not remember when he had slept, but he woke up at the sound of a loud bang. Amit jumped up on his bed. "What is it? A gun shot? That Mackenzie has appeared?" the immediate thought came to his mind.

The thunderstorm had stopped. The depression was blown away. Amit could not understand about the source of the sound. He was sure it was the sound of a gunshot.

RAT TAT TAT

Amit's heart beat stopped for a while. Who was knocking at the door near the balcony? Probably that Mackenzie had come to kill him. But why he had come to kill him? He had done no harm to him. Why was he coming from the balcony?

RAT TAT TAT

Again the ghost of Mackenzie was knocking at the door. Amit started sweating. He thought that there no way to escape from the vengeance of the ghost.

"Sir, please Sir, spare me," Shouted Amit. "I did no harm to you. Please spare my life, I promise to leave this bungalow tomorrow morning," Pleaded Amit for himself.

RAT TAT TAT

The cruel Mackenzie would not spare him; Amit was quite sure about it. He had come here with the intention to kill him. He could not be escaped, he would obviously die tonight.

RAT TAT TAT

Amit started crying now. He lay down and stared at the door. Amit had heard the gunshot already.

The police officer broke down the door. Gurung, Tamang and Chhotelal were standing behind the police officer. When they entered the room, they found Amit was staring at the door of the balcony. Fear was found in his eyes. There was sign of tears rolled down his cheeks. His mouth was wide open.

The police officer touched the body of Amit and found he had died a few hours ago.

Last night's storm cleared the depression, and it was bright all over. Chhotelal came in the morning with the assumption that Amit might have another plan to go to different sightseeing. He arrived at the bungalow at 7.45AM and found the door of the bedroom of Amit was locked. He asked Tamang, who also said the same thing. He knocked the door for a few times, but no response came from inside.

Chhotelal thought that Amit might have tired a lot, so he was having a sound sleep or he was a late riser by default. He had no option but to wait. By 8AM Gurung came to work. When it was 10AM, Chhotelal became impatient, after knocking the door for several times. "What a deep sleep this man had!" thought Chhotelal. By 11AM, he started worrying. Gurung rushed to the police station on his cycle. He came along with the officer at 11.45AM in his jeep accompanied by few constables. What the police officer saw, was stated in the earlier paragraph.

The police officer ordered the constable to call in a doctor. This body might be sent to the District hospital for post mortem.

He looked around and found nothing suspicious. No one had broken into the room. All the doors and windows were bolted from inside.

The police officer could not understand why this man who seemed to be around the age of about thirty-five had died and why his face was so frightened to look at.

RAT TAT TAT

Everyone startled and looked at the balcony door. The police officer opened the door with a creaking sound. He looked around and found none.

RAT TAT TAT

He looked up and found a branch of a tree adjacent to the balcony was broken and dangerously dangling, only a portion of it was connected with the tree. With every gash of the wind, the branch was hitting the wooden wall between the door and the window and making that sound.

RAT TAT TAT

The branch again hit the wall. From somewhere, Gurung managed a pole and hit the point where the branch was connected with the main tree. The broken branch fell with a crash.

All of them were waiting for the doctor to arrive. The police officer sat on a cane chair in the balcony. Just before his eyes, the magnificent Kanchenjunga had been glowing in its full glory.

*   *   *

. . . Subhashis stopped. Both Deepak and Anuraddha were staring towards him with their jaws dropped. Finally Deepak spoke "This is really unusual. A modern urban man like Amit died simply out of fear. I found him quite fearless when he planned to stay all alone in an old nearly uninhabited bungalow."

Anuraddha stopped him by saying "Though it is unusual, it is possible. If you are left in a marooned place all by yourself and you are repeatedly told that the place is haunted, this is possible. Fear is such an emotion that it can take its toll even to the strongest heart. Still it's quite heart breaking."

"Hmmm!!" Deepak replied.

Three of them sat in silence for a while. The rain outside was continuing. One by one the street lights were on by now.

Subhashis said "After Sudip da had returned, he contacted Amit's family through our human resource department and informed them about the misfortune. Another shocker waited for us. Amit's family stayed in a satellite city, not very far from Kolkata, but though Sudip da and Amit da were best of friends, Sudip da knew not much about his family. He called up and found that after his graduation, due to some dispute within his family, Amit left his family and settled in Kolkata. His family comprised his parents and his younger sister. He had not contacted or visited his family for the last ten or fifteen years, and stayed all alone in his own flat. Both his parents and sister though tried a lot to contact him and to persuade him to come back; he avoided them and denied their proposal repeatedly. They, on the other hand, in due course of time adjusted to living their life without him stopped contacting him years ago. Just imagine what happened to their mental condition when they had been informed about the death of their son from whom they had not been heard for so long. Was this news really worth to them? The news of death of their son, who detached himself from them for so long, who knows if Amit was already dead for them, dead in their minds, only informed officially few days back. All of us at the office are really shaken mentally by all these recent events. So, somehow this week our office lost its normal corporate behaviour. You can find this week people gathering and discussing in the corridor, cafeteria and other places. You can find empty cubicles, people leaving theirs and other's cubicle and discussing something in hushed voices."

Three of them were again quiet for a few moments. As the evening progresses, the tea bar was slowly filling up, though it was much below average than what they normally found on a Saturday evening. Anuraddha glanced around and said, "Last Wednesday, I heard something similar like this, I heard about how grief and sadness transforms the mind of a person completely, so much they were unmoved even to the most concerning news connected to their lives."

"What was it, tell us?" Deepak and Subhashis asked her.

"Sure; but let us have another round of our beverages." Anuraddha replied.

They again ordered two cups of tea and a cup of cappuccino.

Anuraddha started; "I told you guys about Julie who came to oversee the operation of our branch" both Deepak and Subhashis nodded their heads "She frequently takes us out to lunch, all of us bombard her with questions and she smiling answers each. She actually has too many stories to share and never tires with our questions. On one such occasion last Wednesday, one of us asked her about the life of theirs, post nine-eleven, how they fought back, especially as she was from New York, all of us wished to hear her point of view."

"Instead of giving her view, she told us a story, the story of her best friend."

The waiter arrived with the beverages. Anuraddha picked her cup of cappuccino and started . . .

A NON-WORTHY NEWS!

The phone placed in the living room is ringing loudly. Mariam comes out of the kitchen to attend the phone.

"Hello! This is Mariam Hussein."

"Hey! Have you checked the news?" shouts Julie.

Julie Francis Andrews works with Mariam in the same creative agency. She has been her best friend, her colleague for more than two decades. And now for the past eleven years, she is her only support.

"What's in the news? What's so exciting? I am cooking now." Mariam replies

"It is something of your interest, darling. Or else why should I disturb you."

"Ok!"

"Ok dear, take care"

"Bye."

Mariam replaces the receiver and slowly moves to the kitchen. She shuts down the gas and moves towards the living room, where the television is kept.

Now-a-days nothing interests her. What could be so interesting that Julie has phoned her? Could it be the news about some movie star, or something political! But Julie knows very well that she is not interested in these things. Is it some sort of disaster or natural calamity? At one moment, she thinks to ignore her friend. Whatever be the news, it cannot change her life. She is 52, a widow and staying lonely in this small flat, where she moved a few years back. This small flat near New York is much smaller than her previous flat. But as she stays alone, this flat fits her needs.

Though she thinks she is not going to switch on the TV, but she finds herself that she unknowingly enters the living room holding the remote of the TV with her hand.

Unmindfully, she switches on the TV and moves on to the ABC News channel, where she finds the familiar face of their President. Mariam is stunned by the news scroll. It reads "OSAMA IS KILLED." Their President is saying that at a place in Pakistan, called Abottabad, at midnight, their Navy Seals broke through a huge mansion, where the said Bin Laden was hiding for the past few years. The news channel keeps on flashing the picture of the bearded man continuously. Seeing the news, Mariam is shocked, she cannot stand any longer. She hurriedly sits on the nearby couch.

She keeps on staring at the TV screen, but slowly her mind has been drifted from the current state.

Mariam was born in Afghanistan; her father was a local merchant there. She had an elder brother. Her mother was a housewife. They had a small house in Kabul and all of them were very happy. She remembers when she had just entered her teens; her beautiful country was attacked by an external force named Soviet Union. Suddenly everything was changed. Her elder brother Hassan Ali fled one day. She had heard that Hassan had joined the Mujahedeen to fight for his country. Her father Idris Ali decided to leave this country and to settle in the West. She still remembers that she cried all the night before she had to leave for the new world. She loved her country dearly.

Mariam is stunned by the news scroll. It reads "OSAMA IS KILLED."

She had never heard from her dear brother. Idris Ali landed in New York and with the help of the Afghani community in New York set up a small shop.

Mariam had completed her school and joined the School of Visual Arts. She got the news of her country, which was not very encouraging. After fighting a long battle with the Soviets, her country was taken over by the extremists named Taliban. They had imposed many bans in the country and especially the lives of the women had become very miserable. Those who opposed the Taliban were openly shot and hanged. She hoped her dear brother was still alive and might become a leader of the Taliban. What would be their lives if her father had not fled from their country! Would her dear brother impose the same bans on her, whom he cared so dearly!

While she was taking her courses at the School of Visual Arts, she fell in love with a guy, named Mansoor Hussein. He was born in New York and a true liberal Muslim. Idris Ali also liked him and accepted him as his son-in-law. Mansoor was a few years older than Mariam and was a Finance MBA. Mariam also developed a deep bonding with an American girl, named Julie. She was her first friend in this foreign country, her neighbour. They shared the same school, college and now the workplace. She had a strange bonding with her and treated her as her sister. Mariam married to Mansoor soon after the completion of her graduation from the School of Visual Arts and they moved to a big studio apartment near Manhattan.

Mansoor till then bagged a top post of Financial Advisor in a prestigious bank. He had his office in the North Tower of World Trade Centre. Mariam also got a job in a creative agency. Mansoor's parents lived in Sacramento. His father was a police officer there. Mansoor loved Mariam a lot and she was very happy.

Within a year, they had a son whom she named Aslam. They were very happy till that Doom's Day of September.

As always, Mansoor who was then in his mid-forty, went to his office. Aslam had also gone with him. He was a young man and joined last week as a junior trainee in his dad's office. Mariam was the last person to leave the house as there was no fixed in or out time at her office.

But that day was different. That day also Julie rang up and shouted that they were attacked. Mariam heard a faint thud a few moments earlier. She switched on the TV and witnessed the most horrifying pictures which she had never seen before. A plane dashed to a tower of the World Trade Centre. The World Trade Centre, where her husband and her son were, was demolished. She thought to take the car, but dropped the plan thinking about the traffic. She had to rush there as soon as possible.

There was chaos everywhere. She heard about the second attack and thought this could not be an accident. It was a planned attack; she was stopped at a distance from the Twin Towers by the NYPD. Screaming sirens of the fire-fighting engines and ambulances passed her. She started praying to Allah for the safety of Mansoor and Aslam. She looked in awe at the burning towers. The place was slowly filling up with thick, black smoke of debris. She saw some people were jumping from the windows. While the North Tower was tumbling down, she fainted.

She gained consciousness in the hospital. She found her father and Julie were beside her bed. Her father had a gloomy face and Julie's red eyes proved that she had cried a lot.

"Where is Mansoor, where is Aslam?" Screamed Mariam.

"No news of both." Idris Ali replied, "But we are in constant touch with the police and the Rescue Department."

Till today, she has got no news of Mansoor and Aslam. Their names had been put into the missing persons list and thought to be buried under the debris of the Twin Towers.

Her world had changed. Suddenly she was all alone. The man of her life and the soul of hers were lost. Within a few hours, her world was crushed in front of her eyes.

But why?

What was the fault of her husband and her son, and of those thousands of innocent people along with them?

Later, she had heard of an Arab millionaire, who is now the head of the extremists, controlling her motherland, named Osama Bin Laden, who was the brain of the terrible attack.

That bearded man might be the boss of her missing brother, if he was still alive. Might be her brother was involved in planning those attacks. What would Hassan think if he comes to know that he had ruined his sister's family!

For nearly a year, Mariam confined herself in the flat. Idris Ali had visited her many times and asked to come and stay with them, but she declined. Julie regularly visited her, she insisted her to join the office, to come out, to meet people. But she had lost all interest to the outside world.

There had been days when Mariam did not take her bath, did not cook and took her meals.

Their President declared war against terrorism and started bombing on her motherland.

A year had passed and she slowly recovered from the shock. Though she hardly reflects the previous Mariam, she felt an urge to come out of the mourning state not only for the rising bills which needed to be paid, she came out to survive herself. She had spent many a sleepless nights, cried too much. Bank authority sent her notices for the pending instalments of the flat. Mariam decided to return the flat of her beloved husband to the bank and move to a smaller flat. This flat had too many memories of her husband and her son. Her whole married life and Aslam's short lived life was spent in this place. She could still hear their voices, their giggles when she closed her eyes. Besides, she was unable to afford the flat in her own income.

So, finally she decided to leave the flat. She was in tears when she handed the keys over to the Bank officer.

She rejoined her office. She was grateful to Mr. Todd Martin, her boss, to retain her job. She did not care whether her boss had given her the opportunity out of sympathy or for the need of her creativity. Actually, she does not care for anything anymore. She now realizes that she does not miss them bitterly as before.

She only speaks to Julie now-a-days, who floods her with all sorts of news. Mariam understands that Julie only tries to make her normal again. But Julie on the other hand also realizes that Mariam has little interest in anything.

Many a things happened.

The Taliban were defeated. That bearded man had escaped the hands of America. Afghanistan was destroyed and America has got the first Black President.

Mariam is also coming back to her normal life, but her emptiness has not filled

She still spends sleepless nights. Those horrifying memories still wakes her up from her sleep. She frequently has a nightmare that Aslam and Mansoor were crying for help from deep underground.

Now, while watching the ABC news bulletin, her memories dazzle like lightning.

The President's declaration of triumph over terrorism means nothing to her now. Can this so called triumph bring back her beloved Mansoor, her dearest Aslam? Can this bring back those eleven lost years?

No. This news is no more important to her. What is lost is lost forever

She now realizes that her phone is ringing.

Who could it be?

She switches off the TV. She moves to the kitchen and empties the food in the bin. She has no appetite.

A streak of tear drops from her left eye.

She moves to the bedroom.

The phone again started ringing.

*　　*　　*

. . . Anuraddha finished her story and looked towards her two friends; both of them were now staring vacantly towards the window, they were in deep thought. The rain didn't seem to stop, going on continuously.

Finally Deepak turned towards her and said, "Really very touching, sometimes life plays such games with us, we really cannot understand."

Subhashis replied "If you lose someone so close, someone you love so much; your whole world comes tumbling down. You will lose all interest in life. No matter how much excitement happens around you, you will find yourself detached from everything. Time may heal your wound, but I believe that there are some losses which never fill up. The memory of the person will shift from your focus in due time, but whenever there is some slight reason, some weaker moments of life; those painful memories will bounce back."

Anuraddha added, "Suppose we lost someone whom we loved so dearly, our mind, after the initial shock, will try to adjust itself by shifting its focus from the pain temporarily, but we don't realise that our mind smartly saves that memory. Only we thought that we have overcome that phase and ready for facing the world with new enthusiasm. But the moment we are brought face to face with something which connects us with the one we lost, our every enthusiasm evaporates and we realise that how much we still miss that person. Say for example, a few years back I lost one of dearest relatives whose place was just next to my parents. You guys know I was depressed for a long time in that period; I even became irregular in this meeting. But slowly I recovered, started meeting people, and tried my best to come back to my normal life. After few months I found that I was again behaving normally and thought I had recovered from my phase of depression. But due to some reason I started avoiding the area where my relative lived."

"Well last Sunday I had to visit the mall near my house for some urgent shopping. I normally take a rickshaw and that evening also did the same, but due to some religious ceremony I found all the roads were blocked except the one which passes through the area where my relative lived. The rickshaw puller, before I realised, turned the rickshaw and took that road. That few minutes were like hell to me. All my memories bounced back and that whole evening was spoiled and I spent it in my old depressive state. I even had a row with one of my colleagues, who happen to be my best friend at the office. Though I have recovered quickly this time and apologised and made up with my friend, I realised that no matter how much we try to run from our memories, it will never leave us." Anuraddha paused.

"As I haven't experienced like this, I cannot exactly feel how you felt that evening, but I can understand what you meant to say Anu." Subhashis replied to her.

"Thanks Subha." Anuraddha smiled and patted him.

Both of them found Deepak was in deep thought. Subhashis shook him by his shoulder and said "Hey buddy; where are you, what happened?"

Deepak seemed to be suddenly bought back from a deep sleep, but he smartly recovered and said "No, no, it's ok. I was listening to Anu, but her experience suddenly reminded me about what I heard from Ruku di last Sunday. That time it was not totally clear to me, but after hearing the Mariam's story it is much clearer to me".

"What is Ruku di's story; well if you have no objection then you can share with us." Anuraddha told Deepak.

"No, no." said Deepak "I have no objection. The only thing is that it is quite a long story."

"Both of us can spare few more times. Though the weather makes it look gloomy outside, it's only 7PM. We can spend a couple of hours more. So Deep, go on." Subhashis replied. Anuraddha nodded and give her consent.

Deepak looked towards the rain drenched city from the big glass window and commences . . . .

THE SIXTH PASSION

It was 6AM. Sneha was sitting on the veranda of her government bungalow. Though it was middle of October, in her hometown in Kolkata it was still hot and sweaty but in this Chhattisgarh region of the country, the mornings were chilly. As the day progressed, it became warmer but locals were predicting that this region would experience record cold in the ensuing months. Sneha was wearing a light shawl over her housecoat; she didn't want to fall prey to this changing weather.

Budhiya, her servant had already placed a cup of hot tea in the small cane table in front of her. She took a small sip from the hot beverage and put it down. A white envelope was also lying on the table. Sneha didn't sleep last night. She was engaged in thinking about the events occurred since she came here. When the night was nearing to its end, she typed the letter. After many times of deletion and retyping it, she finally agreed on the draft, took a print out and put it in the envelope. She would submit the letter in the morning.

But, what was in the envelope?

Well! Before I tell you, let me tell you the whole story and the reason behind the letter. Hope you don't mind.

{1}

The moment Sneha had put down the receiver, she started trembling, suddenly she felt that she was emptied from inside. Juthika, her friend called up and said that the result of their MBBS examination was declared and they were going to check it immediately, and whether she would join them. Sneha was a good student throughout, she scored quite a high rank in her medical entrance examination and in her medical college she was always among the top. Her professors had high hope for her and they were sure that she would as always come among the tops. But she, herself always had these sorts of effects, before every result declarations. What if she had made some terrible mistakes in the answer sheets, what if she missed some points to answer, what if she completely misjudged an analysis and came to a different conclusion which failed to impress the examiner. At one moment, she planned to hide under the bed, but thought it would be childish and decided to meet her fate.

Sneha, the second child of Dr. Ambarish Gupta and Mrs. Shila Gupta, stayed near Hazra Road in South Kolkata. Her father is a well-known heart surgeon in the city. They also have a son named Angshuman Gupta, who is presently doing his Masters in Chemical & Environmental Engineering from Yale University, after completion of his B. Tech from Kharagpur. Their family has an equal mixture of both doctors and engineers, and as Ambarish's son is an engineer it is expected that his daughter will pursue her career as a doctor. During every family get together and in Durga Puja, their family expectedly divides into two zones of doctors and engineers

Her father was sitting in the drawing room with her uncles and few of her father's colleagues. All of them had a stiff face and were talking in a low voice.

and there is a mood of teasing each other and pulling each other's leg.

When she entered the medical college, the first person came rushing towards her was Juthika. She gave Sneha a tight hug, congratulated her and told her that she knew Sneha would score this good. A couple of professors and many of her friends congratulated her in the corridor. Everyone was happy with her result. Tukiram, the housekeeping supervisor came and told her that the principal wanted to meet her. She rushed towards the principal's office.

She was greeted by the Principal of the medical college, Dr. Indrajit Ray, she was always his favourite and he was also a close friend of her family, especially of her father but he also has a good rapport with a few of her uncles, who are also renowned doctors. He liked her as her own daughter and her good academic track record won a place in his heart permanently. He told her that he had already called her father and gave him the good news. Dr. Ray enquired about her plans and insisted that she should pursue further studies. He suggested her to some good foreign universities such as Medical School of the Harvard University, Yale School of Medicine, as her brother was also at Yale and also she could consider the prestigious School of Clinical Medicine of the University of Cambridge. He could recommend her name in any one of them.

But Sneha had other plans which she told to her principal and she pleaded him to help her in this matter. Dr. Indrajit Roy was shocked after hearing this. He tried to put her in the sense and repeatedly asked her to consider his suggestion. But finally he had to give up in front of the firmness of Sneha. Sneha finally was able to convince him and Dr. Roy promised to help her though he told her if she would ever change her mind she should let him know immediately and he would arrange whatever suitable for her.

{2}

The atmosphere inside the house of the Guptas resembled that someone's death had occurred there. Sneha's mother was crying; her grandmother locked herself in the room used for puja; her father was sitting in the drawing room with her uncles and few of her father's colleagues. All of them had a stiff face and were talking in a low voice. Ambarish was holding his face down in his palms. A few moments ago Angshuman called up and he too like others was upset with the decision of his sister's. He even tried to talk sense to his sister but failed. He even scolded her. Everyone was telling her that she was ruining her own career and insisted that she should change the decision. After a while, one by one all of them left.

After a long time Sneha came to the drawing room. Her father was still sitting in the same position. Sneha slowly came in front of her and called him.

"Papa!"

Ambarish did not reply or took his face up from his palms.

"Papa!" "Please talk to me." "Please listen to me, don't be angry with me."

Slowly, Ambarish looked towards her daughter. Sneha's eyes filled with tears.

Seeing her face, Ambarish's anger melted a little and after a long time he talked to Sneha. "When Dr. Ray called me up and told me about your achievement, it was one of the best moments of my life. But it was perhaps the shortest lived happiness of me. When again your principal called me and told me about the decision, my world was tumbling down."

"Why, Ruku (pet name of Sneha) you have taken such a decision?" asked her father. "I have so many dreams regarding you. Babin (pet name of Angshuman) has taken up engineering. Though I have never objected to his decision, but always wanted one of my children should pursue the field of medical world. Though, on the other hand I never dictated to you about your career. I always supported you in your every decision of life. When you told me that you wanted to sit for the medical entrance examination and not the engineering, I became very happy. You have always been a very good student and I always have a great hope for you. And I should appreciate your achievements. But your decision of today really shook me up. Your good academic record will be wasted in such a decision. You should follow your principal's advice."

"Papa! I know I have hurt you. I am really very sorry for it. Please believe, I have no intention to do it. But Papa, since my childhood days, I always have a dream to do something for the less fortunate people. You know how I helped poor kids of our locality with books, clothes, etc. when I was in school. I wanted to become a doctor only to help those who need it the most. There are so many things to do for the less fortunate ones, if a doctor can't help them, then who will. What they need today is a good and dedicated doctor, so that they don't have to be at the mercy of the quacks, they shall have proper nutrition, medication, their wife can give birth to healthy babies, and their babies can grow to a healthy boys and girls and built a better society for themselves. I have studied about the conditions of the government-run hospitals and health centres in the Jharkhand and Chattisgarh areas for the last few years, and found how those portions are continually neglected. Isn't it our duty as a doctor to help the people, who need it the most?"

"But Ruku, you can help them after you have completed your masters. You can then also help them. Why ruin your career."

"You know very well, that if I complete my masters from some foreign university, then also this same situation will occur. Then also I will be questioned that why I am ruining my career, my future. Can you promise Papa, that then I won't have to face these questions, what I am facing today? Will everyone then let me do what I want to do?" Sneha threw these questions towards her father.

Ambarish couldn't reply, only gave a nod and lowered his head.

"And Papa" continued Sneha "If I really be a failure then I can always come back and listen to the suggestions to go for higher studies. But please let me at least try once."

"But Ruku, why do you want to go to the Jharkhand area? You know about the Maoist turbulence there. Those villages are mostly controlled by the Maoists. There are so many news of abductions, killings, blasts, etc. come to us every day from those areas. If you really want to help the village people then you can go to state owned hospitals of Midnapur, 24 Parganas, Murshidabad and various other places. Why are you planning to go to so far away?"

"Because Papa, the tribal villages of those areas are much more neglected than the districts of Bengal and I have studied about those places a bit. I have little bit better knowledge about the conditions of those places than our districts."

Dr. Ambarish Gupta no more argued with her daughter. He got up from the chair and put his right hand on his daughter's head and said. "Take care Ruku. God bless you. Though your Mom and brother will never understand and approve this, but you go and live your dream."

{3}

Sneha took a lung full of breath. This air was so pure and pollution free. Sneha reached this small village near Kuwakonda in Dantewada district in the morning. Her principal, Dr. Ray had arranged for everything. According to her wish, she got an appointment in the government run hospital near Kuwakonda. This was a nice green place and was surrounded by small hills and hillocks and was inhabited by many tribal groups such as Muria, Dhurwa, Halba, Bhatra, Gonds, etc. Before, leaving Kolkata, Dr. Ray told her everything about the place. He told her about Budhiya, her servant cum caretaker, and arranged him to receive her. When Sneha, got down from the bus which she boarded from Raipur, a middle aged man rushed towards her. Checked half sleeved shirt and white dhoti, with a broad smile, he immediately handed her a letter. Sneha, recognized the writing and signature of Dr. Roy, and remembered that he had promised her to write a letter to Budhiya stating her details of arrival. Sneha, smiled back to Budhiya. This man had a peculiar charm in himself, and Sneha immediately felt at ease with this middle aged man. Budhiya took all her luggage and moved towards the white ambassador which bore the name of Gongapal General Hospital on its side. This particular ambassador seemed nearly two decades old to Sneha, still she was happy that the hospital had arranged at least this much mode of conveyance for her.

Budhiya, placed her bags in the luggage space and opened the back door for her. After she had entered, he sat at the front beside the driver. Without any word, the driver, whose name she later learned as Chautram, started the car. Budhiya started talking with her the moment the car started. He told her about lots of things about this place, about the culture, about the people of the area. He told her that this place was mainly inhabited by the tribal people who occupied more than sixty per cent of the population. The literacy rate was also very low in this part of the country. The hospital fell under the tehsil of Dantewada and very near to the border of Andhra Pradesh in the south and west and Orissa in the east. The people of these areas were poor and simple. But since last five to six years, these areas came under the threat of the Maoist movements which really disturbed the peace of the area. Now a day the daily conflicts between the security task forces and those Maoists were hampering the daily lives of the poor tribal peoples. The progress and growth of the state and specially this area was hampering. As this area was very near to the borders of two states it was very easy for them to commit a crime and fled to a neighbouring state and also after committing a crime in those states then often came and took shelter in these areas. He was about to tell something but suddenly refrained and changed the topic and started enquiring about Sneha's family.

Sneha also came about the declining condition of the government run hospital, this facility happened to be the only hospital for many a miles and covered a wide range of area, but the severe crunch of supplies and lack of basic modern amenities were really taking a toll on it. Due to the political instability of the area the staffs of the hospital had also diminished. For quite a long time no good doctor came to the hospital, and whoever came, planned to leave as soon as possible. In the absence of a properly trained doctor, Budhiya treats the patients whoever comes for treatment. Mostly the villagers come with some basic problems, which can be treated with the available stocks. If anyone comes with some severe problem, then they are referred to some other hospitals with slightly better facility, though the condition of the other hospitals and health care centres are not much different from theirs. Around ninety percent of the cases, those tribal villagers hardly come back or go to some other hospitals, but turn to some local quacks or leave their fates in the mercy of their gods. The situation is really bad here. Budhiya was really surprised when he came to know that a young doctor from Kolkata named Sneha had wished to come to their hospital on her own. After seeing this lady doctor, Budhiya became confident that this lady was different from the others. Though she is much younger than the previous ones, she has a strange firmness in herself. Looking into her beautiful face automatically fills one's heart into joy.

In the last part of the journey, Budhiya talked no more to Sneha. He turned and looked through the windshield. Sneha, looked outside the window and enjoyed the beauty of the nature. Nice and small hills, fresh and green everywhere.

{4}

After reaching the hospital, Sneha expressed her desire to see the hospital once before retiring to her quarter. She was prepared for some surprise, for some real setback which is going to shatter her dreams. The condition was exactly the same as described by Budhiya on their first meeting, even worse in some aspects. The first impression of the hospital really took Sneha off guard, she expected it would lack few facilities, but did not expect it to be so bad. The entrance was broken, after the entrance in the left side one could see two cows tied to a tree, munching on their feeds and a stack of cow dung kept beside them. The urine and dung of them made the air filthy.

"They are chowkidar Chuniyaram's." Budhiya replied before being asked.

After walking a bit, she climbed the few stained steps to enter the one storied hospital. The walls were hand painted with campaign pictures of various governments backed health programs like birth control, polio, fight against tuberculosis, etc. But even the coat and condition of the paintings matched with the surrounding atmosphere. There was an outdoor facility with the lack of the most basic amenities with very few medicines and ointments to treat a patient, and completely unsuitable for any sort of emergency. There is a ten bedded facility, which has proper bedding in just two of them, though those also seem to be occupied by patients in ages. When asked about the rest of the bare cots, Budhiya smiled and replied they hardly ever needed, so laying the beds means extra cleaning and maintenance. Patients come here only when they have a fever which they treat with paracetamol, few cases of cut and injury and some cases of childbirth, though most of the tribal people still depend on their "Dai Ma" or midwife for bringing their new born. All the previous doctors who came over here, hardly did anything to change the condition, as their primary goal was to complete the term here and transfer to some bigger and better hospital. It seemed that they were sent for some sort of punishment, which they wanted to complete as soon as possible. She was informed that she was the first doctor, who willingly came to this hospital.

"I have a mountain to climb, if I seriously want to do something to improve this place." Sneha made a mental note.

After the initial disappointing inspection of the hospital, Sneha was ushered to her small bungalow. This place was much better maintained than the main hospital building itself, and though not lavish, liked by her. It has a small veranda in the front and also a small garden. A few seasonal flowers were blooming there. She had the urge to ask Budhiya why this bungalow was much better maintained than the whole hospital, but restrained herself. Sneha, found by this time her baggage already reached there. Budhiya said goodbye to Sneha, but before leaving, told her that her lunch would be given in time and whether she wanted some tea and snacks in the meantime. Sneha smiled and thanked

Sneha, recognized the writing and signature of Dr. Roy.

him. In this small time, a strange bond had developed between them and Sneha was sure she had to depend a lot on this smiling middle aged man, while Budhiya promised to himself that he would protect and help his madam in whatever she wanted.

Even Sneha was very tired from the long journey from Kolkata. She quickly changed her clothes and head for a bath to refresh her. She was pleased to see the washroom as she was a little fussy about the bathroom. She opened a shower; the cold water started feeling her soul.

"I have an uphill task ahead." thought Sneha. "Many a changes need to be brought over here and that task is never going to be easy. There will be so many resistances I have to face. But as long as I am here, I will surely do my portion for the betterment of the people and the area, specially this general hospital."

The water slowly refreshed her.

{5}

A few weeks had passed since Dr. Sneha Gupta; Daaktar Bahin (Doctor Sister) for the locals; started her work at the hospital and very soon she became a likeable figure for the villagers. Though she could not make any drastic change for the hospital, but a very few which was within her capability. The first notable change done by Sneha was to move the two cows of Chuniyaram's and cleared the entrance so that patients should have no problem in coming to and going from the hospital. She made arrangement for Chuniyaram's cows at the backyard near the quarters of the staffs; she also talked with Budhiya if a permanent shelter could be arranged for the cows. Chuniyaram was also happy with the arrangement. Sneha personally inspected over the cleanliness and hygiene of the hospital and it's outdoor. The facility now looked and smelt better from its previous state. She ordered to lay down all the beds, to mend few mattresses, regularly cleaning the bed sheets and pillow covers. She also, immediately put requisition to the state health department for new medicines and replacement of the expired ones. Few medicines were sent a couple of days later, but not all as per her requisition. Though, she was assured by the state health department, that they would send the required medicines soon after a check of stocks and requirement scrutiny from their side. Though Sneha was not happy with this decision, she said to herself to have more patience, as she knew all her wish won't be fulfilled soon. She has to prove herself to the department. The footfall of patients increased a little bit, though it's nowhere near her expectation and she found most of them came out of curiosity to see the new lady doctor as she was later informed that she was the first lady doctor of the area. But she never showed any sign of frustration, disappointment or anger to anyone who came to visit her, even if they came without any purpose. Her sweet face and smile welcome all and they were started liking her and started calling her Daaktar Bahin as I mentioned earlier.

Sneha also visited the nearby villages, talked to village heads, spreading awareness among the village women for safe childbirth methods, about hygiene related issues and how to look after the health issues of themselves and their children. Budhiya, always accompanied her in her village trips and day by day he was amazed and appreciating the activities of this new lady doctor. He was confirmed by then, than the first day of their meeting, that this Bengali doctor could really do something for the betterment of this locality. For the villagers, first time someone from the learned class was really caring for them, till now for them that class comprises of political leaders, police and task force personnel, block officers, post master, station master, etc., but none of them cared for them. Police and political leaders were corrupt to the highest level and while one class always provided them with false promises, the other one ran terror in their areas by raiding their villages every now and then, torturing and picking anyone not even sparing women for interrogation regarding Maoist activity, few of them never returned.

{6}

Nearing a month, after Sneha joined in her post, she had two unusual visitors in her bungalow. One was the local MLA, Sohan Lal Singh, who came with his private armed bodyguards. The presence of armed musclemen really un-comforted her. The MLA came to her with folded hands and told her to inform him immediately if she needed any help from his side. But Sneha, could sense instantly that the man sitting in front of her was wearing a mask and just in a drop of hat, this man would straightaway show his true colour of nature. The unconcealed greedy eyes of the middle aged MLA, was measuring her, and continuously moving over her body. Though, she was very well accustomed with these sort of looks, this MLA was way ahead of all. His pan chewing stained smile was a complete parallel of his lustful eyes. She heaved a deep sigh of relief after the MLA left, and made a mental note not to come across this person till the worst of the situation arrived. Later, she heard lots of stories about this MLA from Budhiya, who swears quite a few times while telling his stories, and Sneha was not at all puzzled that she judged the person correctly.

The next day, after the visit from the MLA, Sneha had her second unusual visitor. This time she was visited by an officer of the special task force, whose name was ASP Mohan Singh. This person was a complete contrast of the previous visitor. She didn't know what happened, but she felt quite comfortable in the presence of the young ASP, who might be just a few years older than her. ASP Singh discussed with her in various matters of the area, how slowly this particular area of this country was slowly becoming a hell of political unrest, how poorest of the villagers were getting attracted towards the rebel ideologists and slowly getting detached from the mainstream. There were so many things need to be done in this region but in reality nothing was done for the poor of this region. How, the ministers, the political leaders used the simplicity of the villagers to fill their vote banks and completely forgot them after they were elected for the assembly or the parliament. How the Maoists leaders were taking this as an advantage and brain washing the simple villagers and turning them against the system for their own benefits. Sneha found how his view about this region matched hers though their approach towards the solution differs. But Sneha was not ready to bring out their difference in their first meeting. ASP Singh also told his stories about few encounters between his task force and the villagers

turned Maoist, how few years back he felt sorry to open
fire to the badly armed villagers who mostly fought with
spears, bows and arrows. But things inside the jungles
were now changing rapidly. The rebels were now getting
trained in modern ammunitions and they were getting
hand in Kalashnikovs and grenades, and even a few
mortars and rocket launchers. The nature of rebels were
also changing, now a days there were more outsiders
in the jungle who were more well trained than their
predecessors, maybe even they were trained abroad by
the enemies of the nation. He also mentioned about one
particular leader, who was heading a large group of rebels
for the last few years, and gained a prominent stronghold
in the area. He was fearless and notorious. The task force
also had very little information about him, only that he
was in his mid or late tweens might be of the same age
of ASP himself. Even most of the captured rebels either
knew less of him or declined to give more information
about him. His group was responsible for most of the
recent terrorist activities of the area, including looting
goods trains, kidnapping, raging police stations and
killing both task force personnel and their informers.

Sneha also came to know about ASP Singh's
background, how he came from a poor background, his
father was a farmer, his housewife mother, how against
all odds he cleared is IPS examination.

She didn't realise how time passed, before ASP
Mohan Singh asked permission to leave. Before, he left
he also told her to inform him immediately if she needed
any help from his side but this time Sneha's mental note
was completely different from the previous day. She
would be more than happy to meet him soon and hoped
even ASP Mohan Singh would feel the same way. He

gave her a firm handshake, which indicated both the mental and physical strength of this man. Long time after he had left, Sneha kept on thinking about their first meeting. That night she dreamt about him.

{7}

Three months passed since Dr. Sneha Gupta had joined this small Gongapal General Hospital. More and more people were coming to the hospital, even from distant villages people were coming for treatment. The hospital beds, which just a few months back, were empty, now filled with patients. Freshly washed bed covers and pillow covers, bright lighting, everywhere there was a smell of freshness and hygiene. The outdoor was full of activity. The state health department was quite impressed with the improvement of the hospital; even the health minister had a talk with Sneha. The medicinal supply was improved and regularised. Health minister even promised a visit to the hospital in near future. Sneha was preparing a report to present in front of the health minister which would focus on increasing staff members, more facility for the patients, even permission to open a small operation theatre.

Sneha's friendship with ASP Singh also deepened; he visited several times in the last few months. They even jointly visited the villages, listened to their problems, talking to the village heads, trying to solve what was within their reach or if not possible forwarding it to the respective departments. Sneha also invited ASP Singh, whom by now she called by his first name, for dinner in her quarter quite a few times. They talked about a lot of things in those evenings. Mohan told her about his recent encounters with the Maoists, even a few tales about their leader. Anyway, Budhiya was also very happy about this friendship between his madam and the ASP. He prayed silently for them.

That evening, Mohan was supposed to come for dinner, but he telephoned at the last moment and cancelled telling he had some urgent work. Sneha thought, again he must have to go to some encounter with the Maoists. Previously also in a couple of occasions, he had cancelled their appointment. The next day he came and apologized, and told her why he couldn't make it. She was really happy with this friendship. She told Budhiya to put back the food in the fridge, after serving her. She prayed to God for his safety.

When she first heard the BANG at the door, she was still in her sleep; she initially could not understand what time of the day it was. But repeated harsh banging startled up from her sleep. When she came near the drawing room, she found Budhiya was already standing by the door. His eyes were a mix of fright and surprise. The banging continued, Budhiya looked towards her, Sneha nodded to open the door.

Five armed young men rushed inside the room. Looking into them Budhiya shrieked and kneeled down with folded hands. Even Sneha was taken aback by this sudden event; she stood her ground and looked sternly towards them. One of them is holding an automatic Kalashnikov, two of them had country made rifle each, and the rest two had two long knives in their hands which they immediately put inside. They had unkempt hair, unshaved beard, red and fierce eyes, dirt all-over, unclean dress, Sneha needed no introduction that who they were, but why they were here was her question.

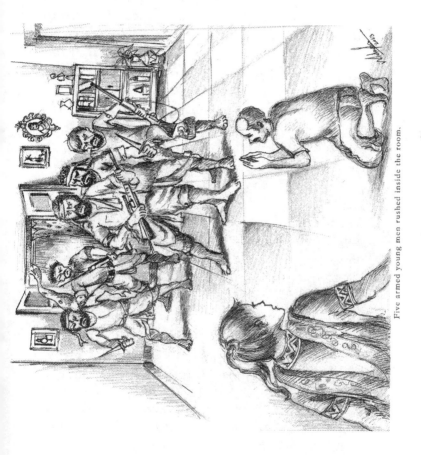

Five armed young men rushed inside the room.

"Daaktar Bahin, you have to come with us." The Kalashnikov bearer roared.

"Why?" Sneha firmly replied.

"Why should I go with you? And why you all are here in this hour of night?" "And by the way, don't you know how to talk to a doctor, especially when the doctor is a lady." This time she raised her voice and sternly asked the group. "And how dare you all fling your weapons at me?" The last line she said looking straight towards the Kalashnikov bearer.

Her firmness and boldness immediately forced the group to lower their weapons, moved aside the knives from sights and lowered their heads. Only the Kalashnikov bearer looked towards her and spoke, but this time his voice changed completely.

"Sorry Madam. My name is Ramuna. Actually we are in a problem that is why we have acted rudely. We all are under tremendous pressure. Please try to understand and forgive us." He told in local accented Hindi.

"We know you are a good doctor, one of our comrades is severely ill, please you have to help him. Sorry, to come to you like this, but you are our only hope. Please come with us to save our comrade." Ramuna told to Sneha.

Budhiya was still shaking and crying.

Sneha's immediate conscious mind asked her not to listen to these men and throw them out of his bungalow. She immediately thought about Mohan, if she could by any means contact him, if he had not cancelled tonight's dinner. But the doctor in herself started reminding her about the duty. She was a doctor first, and she should attend to anyone who would approach her. She remembered about the oath she took when she became a doctor. She decided to go with these men. Though she could not deny the numerous possible dangers she would have to face if she agreed to go with these Maoists. She might not see her dear one's ever. Her papa, mama, her brother Angshuman, all her friends, Mohan, she could never meet anyone of them. But still, decided to go with them. She also thought she would have to face legal problems if she would agree to go and help the Maoists. But she had made up her mind and didn't have time to think all these consequences.

"Ok, I will go with you." Sneha replied this small one liner.

"Nooo" cried Budhiya.

Someone shouted him to shut up.

"Thank you, Daktar Bahin. Thank you very much." Ramuna replied with a tone of gratitude. "You saved us. We will never forget your help"

"I will go with you, but I have one condition." Sneha told their leader. "I will not go alone with you. Budhiya will come with me."

Budhiya looked towards her with tear filled eyes.

"Sure Madam! We have no problem with it." Ramuna replied.

They prepared to leave in a short while. The party of the Maoists, Sneha and Budhiya left the house.

{8}

It had been quite a few moments since they boarded the old jeep of the Maoists. Before boarding they had blindfolded her and Budhiya. Though Budhiya did not approve this but had no chance as Sneha did not protest. Now she was feeling adventurous about the whole thing and was ready to face the unknown. Budhiya was sitting quite beside her, he might be asleep and her medical bag was on his lap. The leader Ramuna was sitting in the front, and all the other Maoists were at the back of the jeep. No one was talking inside the jeep still she could sense their urgency to reach the destination. She could understand at one point that they had left the main road and were going in the jungle, might be through a trail. She was unhappy that she had been blindfolded, as she was missing the journey through the jungle at night. A strange quietness was all over. The sound of the jeep's engine, crushing sound of twigs under wheel and continuous bumps were their companion throughout the journey. Though she was not sure about the exact timing, it could be anything between 30 minutes to 45 minutes; the jeep came to a halt. They were asked to get down and made to walk through the jungle. She could sense that they were moving in a row. Surely, Ramuna was leading accompanied by another Maoist, she guessed through their chatting in the Telegu language. She was behind them, followed by Budhiya, who kept on cursing his luck and praying to God. The rest of the Maoists might be behind Budhiya as she could not hear or sense them. After walking like this for five to seven minutes they were asked to halt. She could feel the presence of many other persons here. They must have reached the destination, but she had no idea in which state they were currently. After a while, their respective blindfold was taken off. She felt completely dark at the beginning which was slowly adjusted and she could see well. They had reached at the camp of the Maoists. Surrounded by some 15 or 20 men, most of them were carrying arms of some kind or other. She was surprised to see a few women among them also. All of them seemed a little worried, she glanced sideways and found Budhiya standing white faced beside her.

They were immediately led to a small temporary hut. Only Ramuna accompanied them. Inside the hut there was only one small kerosene lamp. A bearded man was lying in the cot, which was an exact similarity with the hut. Two men were standing beside him with worried faces. The man seemed to be in severe pain and breathing heavily.

Sneha, acted immediately and sat beside the man, and asked them to show his wound. It was surely a bullet wound, just below the ribs, moved upwards. A rather nasty and deep cut, but the bullet was not inside the body. This man had lost a considerable amount of blood, she immediately ordered for some hot water. The wound needed to be cleaned immediately. She ordered Budhiya to prepare for stitching the wound. The waiter appeared immediately, she cleaned the wound and pushed a couple of injections to stop infection and locally anaesthetise the spot before stitching. After completion, she covered and bandaged the spot and prescribed some medicines.

She was unsure how they would arrange for medicine at night in the middle of the jungle. But, Ramuna took the paper from her and immediately handed it to another person standing outside the hut. Sneha could feel that the man ran straight away.

"That's all I can do." Sneha told to Ramuna. "Have to wait to see the effect of the antibiotics. I also warn that he may show signs of fever. You have to treat him for that. I have written all the necessary medicines. Use them as instructed."

"I need to wash my hands and prepare to burn the stuffs used for surgery." Sneha now instructed Ramuna.

Ramuna, who had not uttered a word for quite a long time, immediately apologised and arranged whatever asked by Sneha. She was accompanied by a girl of 17 or 18 years of age. "Such a young age to join the rebels! What was I doing in her age? Might be having fun with friends, watching movies, going to coffee shops, merry making, preparing for exams. In those years, was it ever occurred in her mind about the conditions of these peoples? In her own country, there could be a girl of her age, who put down books and took up arms to fight her Government."

No, she couldn't remember.

While Sneha was washing her hands, Ramuna kept on staring towards her. "What a mental strength this young lady has" thought Ramuna.

Under these circumstances, he had seen many mature and powerful men to collapse mentally. Till today, whoever they had abducted—be it political leaders, businessmen, government officers for ransom, government favours, releasing captured comrades and various other reasons cried. They shouted, pleaded and finally accepted their fate and waited for their release. Most of them slowly succumbed to loneliness and kept to themselves unless they were released after the demand was met or they had to meet the unfortunate end if the demand was neglected. Though, the latter case was witnessed only twice by Ramuna. But this lady was different. She, not for a slightest moment shown any sign of weakness or lost her control. She had bravely handled every situation, looked straight towards their eyes and talked. She even instructed them to carry her orders. Even, in the time of the stitch, she was terrific. Even now while she was cleaning her hands, she didn't let her self-confidence fall. From that time onwards Ramuna started respecting her.

"Don't you ask your guests even for a cup of tea?"

Ramuna was jolted from his self-absorbed state. He found Doctor Sneha standing in front of him wiping her hands. When his mind had drifted from the current state, he could not remember. He apologised again and moved towards the make shift kitchen.

{9}

It's around 7AM, Budhiya and Sneha were returning in the same jeep in which they came. Sneha, was sitting near the window, but this time she was not blindfolded. Though, they had put on a cloth over Budhiya's eyes. Sneha, kept on staring outside through the jungle. Before, she came here she had no idea how green the forest could be. A narrow track trailed through the jungle with old saal trees on both sides. How old this jungle could be? Thought Sneha. The humming of the jeep was piercing through the silent jungle. She could smell the freshness and greenery everywhere. She was recalling whatever happened to them in the last few hours.

Ramuna arranged tea for all. Sneha and Budhiya joined by Ramuna and few of the Maoists, Sneha guessed all of them hold higher rank than others present in the camp. Most of them thanked her to save the life of their commander. She faintly smiled to them and kept on listening to them. Though, she could not make out what exactly they were saying as they were talking in local language, but she could guess that they were talking about. They were talking about their recent encounter with the forces. How the force suddenly attacked them and they had lost few of their brave comrades and injured their comrade. She was shocked when she heard the name of Mohan Singh. She could feel the anger between them while they uttered the name of her friend ASP Mohan Singh. She tried her best to keep a straight face and closed her eyes when this discussion is going on, so that no one could guess what was going in her mind.

"Oh! My God! Where have I landed? Was Mohan leading the attack on these rebels? Is this the reason he was unable to come this evening for dinner?"

She just saved the life of a Maoist commander who might have been shot by her dear friend Mohan.

While she was thinking all these, a man came and told Ramuna something. He turned towards Sneha and asked her to join him in the hut. She came inside and found the man slowly coming to consciousness. Though, he was very weak and in pain, he was twitching his face and slowly grunting as if he was saying something. She was also surprised to find the medicines she ordered kept in a low stool beside the man, their commander. She came near the bed; hold his hand to feel his pulse. Put her hand on his head, throat, checked his eyeballs. He was moving his lips and saying something which she couldn't make out. She lowered her head near his lips and could make out only two words.

"Thank you!"

She raised her head and turned towards Ramuna and told him that their commander was out of danger now and instructed him about the medicines. Then she turned her head towards their leader and said: "You are out of danger now. The pain will be there for quite a few days. Keep taking the medicines; I have instructed Ramuna in details." She then turned towards Ramuna and without a blink ordered him: "This is the best I can do. Do; send someone to pick me up after one week. AND DON'T BLINDFOLD ME EVER." The last line she uttered with a severe firmness in her voice. She could sense, even the injured bearded man trying his best to listen her. She rushed out of the hut. Ramuna kept on staring towards her, his jaws dropped.

Ramuna came out of the shock and joined her outside the hut. He was surprised about what he heard just now. He came and apologised about the blindfold and promised that she would not be blindfolded in her return. And, if his commander ordered she would never be blindfolded. But, they would have to blindfold Budhiya, as he was a local and might recognise their trail and become a threat to them. But he assured that both of them would be safe as long as they would co-operate with them. Sneha agreed.

She then told him, she wanted to leave soon, as there was nothing left for her to do. She asked Ramuna to make necessary arrangements.

While the jeep left, Ramuna kept on looking towards it for quite a long time. He had never seen such a person in his life. Her mental strength really forced him to admire her. This Bengali lady doctor was gem of a person. And how young she was!!

The jeep bumped against something and Sneha was brought back from her thoughts. The jeep was nearing the Gongapal General Hospital.

{10}

Mohan was sitting opposite Sneha in a stern face. The tea kept in front of him turned cold. His lips were stiff but she could make out how angry he was by looking into his eyes. She told him about her last night's story. Well, though not in full but the carefully edited version.

Mohan came in the morning around 11AM. Sneha was still sleeping then, exhausted from last night's excitement. She had a bath and lied down. Initially she could not sleep, but slowly succumbed to tiredness. She was awakened by Budhiya, who informed her that Mohan Sir had arrived. She was surprised not to find any trace of tiredness on him. Gesturing through her eyes she asked whether he told anything to Mohan regarding last night's incident, he assured by slightly nodding his head that he had not.

She arrived sleepily in the drawing room and found Mohan flicking through a recent popular journal which he put down after seeing her. He smiled broadly and come forward to apologise for missing last night's dinner.

"I am really sorry, Sneha. I was called for duty at the very last moment. I could not deny my responsibility. But you know how our duty is."

"It's ok Mohan. I understand." Sneha replied with a huge yawn.

"But we really had a major breakdown yesterday night. We killed quite a handful of rebels and injured their commander. I planned to get him myself, but they somehow able to conceal him and managed to flee. If he is alive, then next time he won't be able to escape from me. I will kill that son of a bitch myself." He banged his fist in his palm.

Sneha's heart skipped a beat. "How will Mohan react if he discovered whom I had attended and nursed last night?"

"We got tips from our reliable source that there would be a gathering of Maoist's at a particular place. They were planning for something big. We just managed to reach the spot before them and started a surprise attack as soon as they were near the firing range. Though they were initially shocked by the attack, quickly recuperated and shoot back at us. Two of my brave soldiers also got injured. But they are now stable after initial first aid. I will ask them to give you a visit."

Mohan took a pause after this. He took the cup containing tea in his hand. When he was talking, Budhiya placed two cups of tea between them.

He took a sip and narrowed his eyes towards her. "You look severely exhausted today. What is the matter? Anyway, I tried to call you up last night after returning to my quarter but you didn't respond."

"Where were you?" Mohan asked.

So, it's finally came. Sneha took a deep breath and tried to relax her nerves. Now she would have to tell him about her abduction. She closed her eyes for a second and began.

When she had completed her story, she looked towards Mohan. She found that he had already put down the barely sipped tea cup. She had omitted what conversation she had with Ramuna and also left the portions where she asked them to bring her back to attend the wounded Maoist. But whatever she had told, it already had enough impression on him.

His expression radically changed from surprise to awe and finally to anger.

Mohan got up from the couch and stood near the window. He looked outside for quite a long time and finally turned his head towards her.

"HOW DARE THEY?" Mohan shouted.

A considerable amount anger shoot from his mouth. He seemed so angry that he would tear open any of the rebels if they would appear in front of him now. He firmly clutched the back of the couch and said "How dare they came here with arms and abducted you and Budhiya and forced you to nurse the very son of a bitch whom I have been hunting for so long. And . . . HOW COULD YOU NURSE A TERRORIST." The last few words he shouted looking directly towards Sneha.

Sneha shivered a little, not primarily because of his anger, but for the very thought about his would be reaction if he found the whole story.

Yes, they are indeed terrorists, anti-establishment forces. But at this very moment after visiting them she thought them as poor and tribal villagers, immensely poor and deprived from the authorities.

Sneha kept quiet for couple of minutes and calmly replied "When I was in front of the wounded, I had no idea that this very person had confronted with your forces. But after looking a wounded person, I had no option than to follow my duty, as you know we doctors also have to take an oath before graduating. Also, I didn't have many options to choose before the armed rebels. What could I do, in the middle of the jungle surrounded by so many Maoists, most of them carrying loaded arms and other weapons?"

"Hmm!!" sounded Mohan and sat on the couch. The cold tea cup was placed in front of him. He didn't say a word for a long time, but Sneha could feel the heat of anger building inside him. Slowly he rose and told Sneha that he had to move now. He would send the officers to meet her soon for treatment.

Before leaving, he promised Sneha that he would not spare a single Maoist in this area. They must have to pay heavily for what they did last night.

He bid goodbye and before Sneha could say anything he left. Sneha kept on staring towards the path he walked. She sighed, and closed the door.

{11}

A few days passed, since Sneha had nursed that Maoist. Though Sneha ordered Ramuna to have her picked from her stay for routine check-up of the wounded, no one turned up that day. She was not fully sure that anybody would show up on that day, as she heard a lot about the discreet operation and movements of the Maoists. When, the day had passed she sighed and thought that she could give the matter a pass. If they turned up anytime later, she would act according to the situation.

In the meantime, Mohan had sent the two task force officers on the very next day of their meeting, who were injured in that night's encounter. Sneha found the bullet injury to them were only superficial, no severe penetration. She released them only after nursing them well, covering their wounds with fresh ointments and prescribing few medicines.

She expected, but Mohan did not contact her since. Though, there were occasional visitors from his office, the purpose of visits was purely official. They primarily came to note down her statement and enquiring about the place where she was abducted. They also asked her if she could remember any sort of landmark which would help the task force to locate the place in the jungle. She told them she was blindfolded and only after reaching the Maoist camp they took off her and Budhiya's blindfold. She screened off the fact that she was not blindfolded in her return journey. She was relieved when she found that Budhiya also kept tight-lipped about her coming back condition. She expected that Mohan would personally interrogate her, but she was also happy that he didn't. It would be once again unfair to tell him half the truth, unfair to lie to him once again. But she was unsure about how much truth she could share with him in future if the Maoists turned up to take her once again to the jungle. She was sure about one thing, and that was Mohan would not take her second meeting with the rebels lightly. She felt the heat inside him when he was even told half of the story in their last meeting. The volcano inside him would erupt next time. How would he treat his friend then? She shuddered in her seat.

Despite all these, she kept on wondering about this sudden avoidance of Mohan and was sure it was due to her attending the Maoist leader. She was unaware what he was up to in this period of absence. On the eighth day, she was anxious for Mohan and started missing him. He was her only genuine friend in this part of the country. She really enjoyed his company. His visits really charmed her up after her hard day's work, and she was sure he also felt the same way.

She also indirectly enquired Budhiya about his whereabouts, but even her most faithful companion could not help her. It seemed natural to Budhiya who even suggested her that he might be too busy with his work as the activity of the Maoists skyrocketed in these areas recently. He also suggested that the ASP Saab was too engaged now days as he might be preparing for a revenge on those Maoists, who had forcefully abducted his best friend. And it's a truth that Budhiya prayed deeply that ASP Saab would really teach those rebels a lesson so that they should not dare this type of act ever in future.

That night while reading a book before going to sleep, Sneha's mind drifted towards her friendship with Mohan. That man really has been a true friend to her. Due to him, she felt quite safe in this district. Whenever she was in need of moral and emotional support, she found him beside her. But is he only a friend to her, or did he expect more from this friendship? Mohan recently told her that he was willing to take her to his ancestral home and introduce her to his mother. Though, he himself showed no inclination or approach towards her except friendship, but girlish sense told her that Mohan really liked her and might approach and propose to her in future. But then what would be her reaction? It would be a lie to her-self if she disagreed that she didn't like him, or miss him if he didn't show up on a promised meeting, but was she ready to take their friendship to a different level. This would be a very difficult decision for her to make, if ever Mohan popped up the question to her. She sighed heavily. But if she would accompany him ever to his ancestral home, she would also ask him to visit Kolkata and introduce him to Papa and Mom whenever he could manage his time.

Sneha might have dozed while reading the book, because while she heard the tap at the door, she was quite unsure about the time and blankly stared for a few moments at the direction of the tap. Then she jerked from her position and opened the door. She found Budhiya with an anxious face and while she looked over his shoulder she found the reason of his concern.

Ramuna had entered and was standing in the hall. Sneha looked at the clock above his head. It was fifteen minutes past one. But this time Ramuna tucked his Kalashnikov in his back. He smiled when he saw Sneha, she smiled back.

"Madam, I have come to take you. As discussed" Ramuna told Sneha. "I didn't come after seven days, as a precaution. You don't know how secretly we have to move in our country. But we kept a close watch on you yesterday and found there was no trap laid for us. So today I personally have come." Ramuna stopped after telling.

"Ok." The only word uttered Sneha.

Budhiya grumbled, muttered something and gave her a disapproving look.

Sneha again opened her mouth. "You have to give me a few moments to change. And this time also Budhiya should accompany me. You have to assure for the safety of both of us." Sneha told while giving an assurance nod towards Budhiya.

"Ok Madam! But I will have to blindfold him. You know why we have to take precautions."

Sneha nodded and went inside her bedroom to change. She closed the door with a bang.

{12}

She stared at the familiar looking hut for a few seconds. She had spent a considerable time inside this hut a few days back, saving the life of a terrorist. Today again she has to face the leader of all the terrorist activities of the area, the most wanted face of the task force. But she had chosen this fate. So, if anything happened, it was her own responsibility. She felt guilty for putting Budhiya's life in danger for her heroism. She thought about Mohan, how offend he would be if he came to learn about this. It could be the end of their friendship or if something more than friendship was going to happen in future. This act could ruin everything. She felt genuinely sorry for her irresponsible decision and prayed to God that Mohan should not ever know anything about this.

Her thought snapped with a sudden crunching sound. Ramuna was coming towards her. He went inside the hut to tell his commander about her arrival. He barely spent a minute or two before coming back to guide her inside. While going inside the commander's hut, Sneha glanced around. The mood of this camp was much relaxed today.

Few of the Maoists were sitting in a circle and hushing something between them, she even heard occasional giggles from them. She saw a couple of women cleaning and oiling few rifles. To her left she found three rebels standing a distance from each other occasionally watching around themselves with their alert eyes, still she could sense their relaxed reflection. In between the second and third guard she found Budhiya sitting on a wooden box. He was handed an aluminium mug surely containing tea. An unarmed but alert guard standing a few feet behind him, any stupid movement from him and Sneha shuddered thinking what would happen to him. But still she found even Budhiya was calmer than the previous day. His blindfold was removed now though he was fixing his sight on the ground near his feet. Sneha moved her eyesight from this middle aged man and once again really felt sad for him, whom she really grown a fond and fixed her vision towards the entrance of the hut.

After entering, her eyes took a little time to accustom with the sudden darkness inside the hut. Initially she could see nothing but pitch dark, but slowly she found a kerosene lamp burning at one corner and slowly a figure of a man starting to materialise before her. She found her patient sitting in the same cot on which she nursed him a few days back. He was wearing a khaki outfit today, with the same bearded face, but might be little trimmed. But unlike the last time, he was staring with a smiling face towards her. His stare had something, something that suddenly skipped her heart beat for a second.

She felt something inside her, something she never experienced.

"Thank You, Doctor." This was the second time the leader of the rebels thanked her. But this time it was a more firm voice than the last time.

Sneha moved a step closer towards him, to see him clearly. His bearded face reminded her of a very familiar face. Inside that dimly lit hut, she also could make out that the person had a pair of strong and intelligent eyes. His eyes looked familiar to him. She was sure that she had seen these pair of eyes somewhere, sometime in the past. But where? She herself was searching for this answer.

The leader extended his hand towards her when she reached out; he took her hand firmly and gives her a gentle shake. "Thanks again Doctor."

"It's perfectly OK. It was my duty as a doctor." Sneha replied though she felt a strange shiver inside her. "What I did would be done by anyone of our profession. So, it's really not a big deal and by the way I am glad to see you recovered. It was really a bad wound, and you lost a substantial amount of blood that day." She tried her best to keep her nerve cool. "Now let me examine your wound." After being satisfied about the progress of healing, she freshly bandaged the area. "Now, I think my duty is over. I don't think you need my service anymore." She moved back a step from him.

The leader of the rebels smiled and asked her to sit on a small stool. While Sneha took her seat, he himself stood-up and in the meantime Sneha glanced around. There was nothing much to describe. Except the cot and a couple of stools, there was a small table on which the kerosene lamp was kept. Beside it there were few medicines surely prescribed by Sneha and the things which missed Sneha's eyes last time but now surprised him were a few books.

"Well Doctor, my name is . . ." He paused for a few seconds, as if making his mind to tell this woman his true identity. "My name is Shivankar Rao, but my comrades and others know me Suraj Ji. I am the sun for them, who gives them light and show them the path." Sneha didn't reply. Shivankar alias Suraj Ji continued, "I know your city very well, as I had completed my engineering degree from Jadavpur University. It was there, where I was introduced to the ideology what I am following today. So, I definitely do have a respect for your city and its people. So, when I heard that someone from that city was coming to this part of the country, which has been obviously neglected for a long time, as a doctor, who was a lady and of such a young age, it really grew my interest."

Sneha tried to say something but he continued sensing what Sneha was going to ask. "Yes! My men were watching you from the very first day. We have to keep a watch on each and every one, especially the new ones, who arrives in this area. You can't even imagine how strong our network is. But, we found your work towards the poor and deprived people of this area is really appreciable. Even whatever you have done in the hospital to bring up its condition didn't escape our eyes."

Sneha was shocked as she heard this man. What was he saying; her every movement was under surveillance! Whatever she was doing or had done was being watched! She suddenly felt like losing all her privacy. She thought about Mohan immediately. This means that these people were quite aware about her friendship with ASP Mohan Singh. She shivered a little. Did she really make a grievous mistake in coming here? What would be the next move of this Maoist leader? He was quite aware that who was behind the action of the task force, now would he take revenge by holding her captive? Or something worse was waiting for her.

She looked towards Shivankar, who at this moment didn't look danger to her. Who was still talking and surely missed her sudden loss of focus and now talking about the problems faced by the poorest people of this area. How neglected they were, how deprived they were for so long, etc. She kept on listening to him, who was now pacing around the small hut, speaking his own mind out in front of this stranger and slowly Sneha found how both their view about the problems of this area matched.

After completing his lecture Shivankar turned towards her. In that dim light she found his eyes were burning. There was a strange plead with his eyes as if he was asking her to agree with him. Shivankar came and sat on the cot. Sneha took a deep breath and looked towards him. She was caught in his eyes; she thought she could not escape these eyes. They were so beautiful, so intelligent yet so strong. Where she had seen these pair before, she had to find this answer soon.

"Well! Your concern towards the poor and backward people of this region is very genuine. Though, I am here for a short time, still I feel most of the things which you have said now. There are many a things need to be done, sure there is a neglect towards them but still I cannot agree with you on the path you have chosen. Whatever you are doing, do you really think you are doing well to the people who are already in deep trouble for so long. Don't you think this path will slowly take them in a more downward journey? In the presence of such a large number of task forces in these areas, you and your people attacking the forces, extortion, kidnapping and even killing, what good will those things bring to them? There is a total stage of chaos everywhere. Every few days there are exchange of fires between you and the administration. Between you and the forces, have you ever considered what the conditions of the villagers are? What they have to face every day? Someone who has nothing to do between you or the forces. Who is going to look after them? You or the forces? Believe me Shivankar the situation is not at all in their favour. I had visited the villagers who are neutral, who have nothing to do between you or the forces, all they want is to live in peace and look over their poor families. Every day they have to live in fear of rounding up either by your men or by the forces. Did you ever think about them? I doubt Shivankar, I doubt!" Sneha concluded herself and sighed heavily.

Shivankar stared towards her and kept quiet for a long time. Sneha could feel his surprise. Several minutes passed between them, none of them spoke a word.

Finally Shivankar sighed "You city dwellers have no idea about the conditions of the poors here. If you really want to feel their problems, accompany me someday. I will show you another point of view."

"Yes, you were right in judging the problems faced by the villagers due to the presence of task forces here and they are also caught between us and the forces. There were times when an innocent villager was captured by forces suspecting him to work for us. Even we also sometimes make the same mistake. But those are the sacrifices they have to bear on their part. A war is going on between us and the administration and everyone have to bear some price. After all, we all are fighting for their cause and right. We are fighting for our own right."

Sneha was going to protest his view and say something, but she was stopped by Shivankar. "Please come and join me outside for a cup of tea."

{13}

The clock was showing 7AM. Sneha was sitting on the veranda of her small residence. Budhiya had gone to sleep. "Poor fellow!" Thought Sneha, "What unnecessarily tension he had to go through due to my heroism."

Before retiring towards his servant's quarter, Budhiya insisted to make her a cup of coffee, but she declined the offer. She didn't want to put any extra burden on him today. Already he had gone through enough for a day. She pleaded him to go to sleep and also told him not to wake her up, if he found her asleep after he was awaken up. She phoned to the hospital and told them not to disturb her unless there was an emergency in which they could not handle.

She then prepared herself a cup of tea and sat on the veranda. Sipping the hot tea, she glanced behind to analyse whatever she had heard and learnt in the last few hours.

After she came out of the hut with Shivankar, both she and Shivankar were offered a cup of tea each by one of the women cadres. Shivankar said something to her in the local language, which brightened the eyes of the lady, she smiled back and replied. Sneha was only sure to hear the name Suraj Ji twice. She could make nothing out of it. After, both of them completed their cups, the lady took away their used cups. He took her towards the group of Maoists, whom she had found previously sitting in a circle and chatting. They suddenly became aware that their leader was coming towards them. All of them stood at attention and gave Shivankar a military salute. Shivankar signed them to be at ease and introduced them one by one to her. She was amazed to find that all of them were educated and completed at least their bachelor's degree; most of them were from a science background. All of them were from a poor tribal background. There was one Maoist named Srinivasan who had done his masters of engineering from a very well-known and reputed engineering college of South India. He was their main land mine expert.

Taking permission from them, Shivankar moved towards the all women group whom Sneha previously found cleaning and oiling firearms. They had completed their job, and now sitting and chatting among themselves, they were now joined by the lady who gave them tea a moment ago and by another girl whom Sneha recognised her as the girl of 17 or 18 who accompanied her on her previous visit while she was washing her hands after nursing Shivankar.

They also stood up when they saw who was approaching them. But unlike the previous group, they didn't give their leader a military salute but all of them stand at attention. Shivankar released them, and like previous group introduced them one by one.

Those two women she found cleaning rifles were Sugandhi and Devika, they were local villagers, their village remains on the border of Andhra Pradesh and Chhattisgarh states. Both of them were from equally poor families whose fathers were day labourers for the local landowners. Both of them had several mouths to feed, still most of the time they were so ill paid or sometimes not paid at all, that their mother as well as the older girls of the family had to sleep skipping dinner. There was severe malnutrition everywhere. The kids had pot bellies due to swollen and inflamed livers; their noses were always running as they had lack of proper clothing. And not only were these two families, condition was similar all over their village. While Sneha was listening to their condition, she visualised the pictures showing the condition of kids in Somalia or other African countries and shivered thinking she could find similar kids in this country also. Till now, she had visited poor families in various villages, she felt sorry for their conditions, but now she didn't know how she would react if she found a whole village full of these types of kids. She heard this was not their only problem; all these people were just ignored by the authority. They were refused to get any place at hospitals, they never tasted any spirit of festivals, and education was a luxury to them. All the basic needs of humanity were simply ignored them; even people from other villages whose conditions were little better, avoided them.

"That is not all." Shivankar told her. He continued by saying sometimes their fathers were forced to work for the landlords of the neighbouring states and they were paid not in cash but for a handful of grains or substandard rice even for a handful of puffed rice. They could hardly protest or complain to anyone. No one was going to listen to them. No police, no politicians were for them, because neither they could pay them a bribe nor these people reflected in the vote bank. So, these people really didn't matter to anyone.

He took a little pause, and looked towards the tea bearer lady. She came to know about her name as Ulupi. She was born in a village at an Andhra village. She was the eldest daughter of the family comprising of four sisters and three brothers. Her father was a hawker at local trains. He died in a train accident when she was only thirteen. Her mother married to her distant uncle who was an alcoholic. Every night there was abuse, beating and later sexual abuse. That man was horrible. To save herself and her younger siblings, she fled with them and started working along with a few of her sisters and brothers as contract labourers on a nearby site. Their contractor was another bully. In one night, to take revenge on her as she had protested and accused him of stealing the money of the labourers and even threatened to report to the manager as well as to go on a strike, he along with his thugs woke them up from their sleep and kidnapped her along with her brothers and sisters to the makeshift warehouse where all of them were beaten severely. The boys were flogged, kicked, lashed and worse happened to the girls. Sparing the youngest two, Ulupi along with her two sisters were gang-raped in front of their brothers. All of their brothers were stripped, tied to poles and forced to watch this barbarism. One of Ulupi's sisters couldn't stand this savagery and died on the spot. Another sister, she later heard, died a few days after. She somehow managed to survive and thus faced more sufferings.

When her brothers freed themselves and helped her to regain consciousness, she somehow managed to go to the local police outpost, after assuring her remaining brothers and also told them to take care of their sisters, to report against the contractor. But her ill-fate was still not over with her. In the police outpost, she faced another round of insult. They hadn't listened to her or recorded any complaint, but instead, informed her that the contractor was a respectable man who called them up and told them that Ulupi had fled with the money of the labourers. Then and there they arrested her and kept her confined in the cell. Where she was repeatedly raped for four consecutive days by all and finally released with a warning not to report this to anyone and told her that she might have learnt enough lessons not to go against the authority ever. When she returned for her siblings she found none of them and was informed that another sister also died from her internal injury. The remaining brothers and sisters fled in terror and no one knew where they had gone. She has still been searching for them.

Sneha, found Ulupi standing with an expressionless face, but her eyes were moist.

Sivankar again paused and smiled towards her and started telling the background of the girl who was with Sneha on her last visit. He told her name was Surmakee and she belonged to the Gondi tribe. She lived near Gongapal. She was little bit educated, but though educated, couldn't change her fate. When she reached the ripe age of fifteen, one day the eyes of the local MLA, Sohan Lal Singh fell upon her. Hearing his name, Sheha twitched his face. She could very well remember how the eyes of this very MLA scanned her body when he had visited her quite a few months ago and how much she disliked him. Anyway that Sohan Lal Singh offered money to Surmakee's parents to send her to his bungalow, and when they declined he threatened them. Sohan Lal left that day, but the threats continued by his pet goons, and one day when she was returning from her school, they kidnapped her in broad daylight. No one dared to protest that day. Going to the police was of no help, because no one had the courage to take any step against the MLA. She was rescued just in the nick of time before her modesty was outraged, by these

Maoists, when her parents contacted them. From that day onwards Surmakee was with them. She now works as an assistant to their accountant named Chiranjeet.

After completing, Shivankar took permission from them and moved near the centre of the camp. Sneha looked towards Budhiya, he stared back and nodded towards her. Sneha was shocked about what she heard. The real life stories of few of the Maoists.

"So Doctor, this is the real story of the people here. You may have your own ideology, your own theory. But that doesn't work in this real world. I have more than thirty comrades with me, and all of them have a story of their own. All of them were deprived at one point or the other by the authority, by your government. I can narrate each one of it to you, but that won't help you much. Whatever you may think about us, we are the real solution for them. We are their only hope. If you don't get anything by begging, just snatch it as it is your right." Shivankar told her.

"But what about all these bloodsheds? There has to be a peaceful solution of it. Will you achieve anything from these killings? The people who are stuck between they are the real sufferers. You have to think about some alternative solution as this war cannot go on forever. It's a fight between the two uneven forces where the poorest of the poor are suffering." Sneha replied.

"No revolution is won without bloodshed. Look at Russia, or France or recently to the Middle East and North African countries, there is always a spill of innocent blood. It is called collateral damage. We have to forget it and see the greater good. These people know that we are fighting for them and they happily agreed about whatever circumstance they have to face." He paused for a while and looked towards Sneha. Again she was caught in his intelligent eyes. His eyes would say a lot of things to her. He seemed familiar to her, but she still didn't make out where she had seen these eyes.

Sneha opened her mouth "Whatever reason you may say, you know I cannot agree with you. And you know it very well. But still I want to ask you, why you are telling me all these things. Why are you actually leaking your strengths? Introducing your men and women, and also telling me what they do for you. You definitely know how dangerous this could be for you and your organisation. As you and your men kept a close watch on me, surely then you know the list of my friends here, I could easily turn you to the forces. Who will be so happy to crush your organisation, then why are you risking so many things only to make me understand your views and agree with you. I could be the reason for your destruction. Then why?"

Shivankar laughed a bit, looked at her curiously and then told "I know exactly whatever danger I may face. I know very well, that you will never ever speak about these things to anyone. Not even to YOUR CLOSEST FRIEND. But let me ask you something, are you acting or you really don't recognise, because if you are acting you are really wasting your time in this profession."

"Now tell me the truth. Don't you really recognise me Ruku?"

{14}

Sneha shrieked and put her hands on her mouth. She was looking hard at this man, how could he know her pet name. Even Mohan didn't know it. No one, after her arrival, called her by that name except on a few occasions when she talked to her parents over the phone.

"But then how did this Maoist leader know her pet name?" She thought.

Sneha's shriek alerted Budiya, who was standing and glancing questionably towards them. Everyone present there also was looking at them. Sneha gestured towards Budhiya and assured everything was fine. She then turned towards Shivankar and looked at him sharply.

"How do you know my pet name? Because I am pretty sure no one in this part knows me by that name. Neither had I myself told it to anyone. Then?" asked Sneha. Her initial shock was now subsidising and now she was more curious than shocked.

Shivankar who was still smiling, stood up and without losing eye contact with her, told her, "So you really couldn't recognise me, though previously I gave you a hint. Well, I wish to say that I am disappointed, but knowing the current circumstances and how the harsh conditions might have changed me completely. I can understand." He continued, "Well, do you remember any friend of your brother when he was preparing to crack the engineering entrance exam" He stopped and tilted his head on one side.

By now, Sneha's eyes popped and jaws dropped. This could not be true. This very person who was standing before her could not be that studious friend of his brother Angshuman (Babin). This could not be that lean and shy South Indian boy who had come to their home so many times when both he and Angshuman were preparing for their joint entrance exam, who called their mother Sheila Aunty and she also liked him a lot. That boy had intelligent eyes, just like this man. But except that, nothing matched. That boy topped every exam while her brother had to be satisfied with the second position. But despite that both of them were very close, which led him to their home several times. He even voluntarily helped her with her Physics and Maths. She relied on him, because her brother was busy with his cricket or football when was not studying, whereas that South Indian boy kept himself away from most of the outdoor sports. He lived with his relatives not very far from their house.

At that age, she adored both his brother and his friend but no one knew she had a secret crush on that South Indian boy. Only that boy knew it. She herself didn't know when she became attracted towards him while she was taking Physics and Maths lessons.

And after both his brother and that boy cracked their respective engineering exams, he had come to their house only once. Then his brother went to Kharagpur and that boy to Jadavpur for their studies and all of them lost contact of each other. Even she herself became busy with her own studies and her dream was to become a doctor. Everyone seemed to forget that boy. Though she herself tried a couple of times to get his news, but when she was asked why she was asking for him, she felt shy and replied it was just out of curiosity and dropped her query.

But she couldn't imagine in her wildest dream to meet him here, in this hostile circumstances.

When that boy studied with his brother, she knew him by the name of Reddy, Venkateshwar Reddy. But how that studious Venkateswar Reddy had become Shivankar alias Suraj Ji? One of the most wanted names for both the task forces as well as authorities. This man resembled nothing except the eyes of her secret crush that they used to call Venkat. She understood then, why Shivankar's eyes looked so familiar to her from the very beginning.

She remembered that day when she, her brother and Venkat went to watch that Dinosaur film. How she gave him an assurance smile when he accidentally brushed against her. How she grabbed his arm when that Tyrannosaurus was rampaging the screen. She even remembered how both of them glanced at each other and smiled foolishly when they caught each other. How he held her hand when her brother went to fetch a tub of popcorn during the interval.

And how could she forget that day. All three of them were nearing their respective exams. Her brother went to beat his stress by playing a football match. Her father was in his chamber and her mother and others were downstairs. That day even Venkat was stressed. Sneha asked his help in a critical mathematical equation, but she sensed that his mind was somewhere else. Instead of solving it, he kept on saying about what would happen if he failed to the expectation of all. He kept on saying about all the negative things about being unsuccessful. Sneha, sensing his tension put aside the books and put her hands on his clenched fists and pressed lightly. Venkat looked towards her. She put her finger on his lips. She rose from her seat and moved close to him and made him stand. Then without thinking anything she kissed him. She could feel about the initial shock of Venkat, but slowly he relaxed and kissed her back. After a moment she found his lips parted and she felt his tongue on her lips. She also parted her lips and their tongues meet. She could not tell how long they were like this, but could sense his grip loosened, and he moved away from her. She opened her eyes and saw he was looking at her tilting his head on one side. Then without saying a goodbye he left. That night at dinner when Angshuman asked her sister why Venkat left so suddenly, she replied, she didn't know the answer.

She was suddenly jolted from her flashback by an approaching crunching sound. She focussed towards the source and saw Ramuna was coming in their direction. She turned again towards him.

"So Venkat? What is this all about? How and why did you become a rebel? You were such a bright student, why did you waste your career, your future to be something like this?"

"It's good to find that finally you had recognised me." Shivankar replied. "To begin with let me tell you first that the Venkat you know was dead. I am Shivankar as I told you earlier. And who told that I really had wasted something by choosing this path. For me this is more important than doing some blue collar job in some engineering firm."

"Well Ruku, I know there are millions of questions arising in your mind which I will definitely reply. But today I think the time has come for you to leave. We will meet again." He nodded towards Ramuna, who led her and blindfolded Budhiya towards the jeep. Shivankar looked at her with thoughtful eyes and returned towards his hut while the jeep left.

{15}

Few weeks had passed since Sneha's second journey back from the Maoist camp. Initially she was in a state of shock after what she had learnt from the camp, after she came to know who was behind the Maoist movement in this part of the country. She was in a dilemma, while she could not ignore the stories of Sugandhi, Devika, Ulupi or Surmakee. She also could not agree to the path taken up by Venkat or hundreds of young bloods like him. Where was she standing now? She could not ignore Venkat, whom she adored and liked secretly once, and even realised recently that her feelings towards him was not weakened. Can she do something? Or she has to watch him be killed one day by another person whom she likes a lot.

She had made a serious mistake by not telling Mohan the complete truth, and now she realised it's too late. Who would show her the correct path?

That night Mohan came for dinner. He was completely unaware about her second trip, and she was in continuous fear about what would happen if he found about it. She tried her best to appear normal in front of him.

He came at 7PM, and was in his normal mood unlike last time. They talked normally. She was glad that he didn't ask her anything regarding her abduction by the Maoists. Budhiya served them dinner at 8PM. Though it was a simple course of dal, sabji, roti and chicken, both of them ate silently. Sneha found though Mohan looked relaxed externally, he was in some deep thought, as if something really was playing in his mind. While Sheha was talking less in the fear that she might reveal something accidentally to him about her experiences few weeks back.

After the dinner Mohan suggested that they should sit quietly for a few moments on the veranda. They sat there, both of them kept quiet for quite a long time. She could sense there was something playing severely in his mind. "What was coming?" thought Sneha.

Finally Mohan talked, "I am really sorry about the way I behaved last time. But such behaviour only shows that how much I care for you. We two are close to each other for several months now, and in these months our friendship only grew stronger. So, the moment I heard how those bloody Maoists abducted you and poor Budhiya, I could not control my anger. I am once again sorry for shouting on you."

"It's ok Mohan. I had already told you. I can understand."

"Thanks Sneha." Before she could say anything, Mohan started "From the very first day I met you, I found you different from others. It really surprised me that being a woman you chose to come here in this politically disturbed place, but previously without knowing you, I thought that you might be some kind of urban hot head, who was forced to come over these areas and who would find out the first opportunity to catch the train back home. But after our first meeting I could really understand how genuine your concern was towards the poor of these areas. You were the first doctor who really wanted to do something positive here. You were the first doctor; these people could rely upon and think her as their own. I liked you from that very beginning."

"Slowly our friendship deepened. I came to know you more clearly. How I found out that both our views natches. I really didn't know when I fell in love with you."

Hearing the last line, Sneha was jerked. Did she hear it correctly? Was Mohan just proposed to her? It's not that she didn't like him also it's not that she wasn't aware that this situation would come to her. She also questioned herself what was she going to reply when this situation would arise. Well, if it was a few weeks back, it would be much easier for her. But right now, just after Mohan's proposal she in a flash, visualized the bearded face of Venkat alias Shivankar alias Suraj Ji.

But for obvious reason she could not let Mohan know about what she was thinking.

"Mohan!! I really appreciate our friendship. Your presence was the only reason that I survived for so long in this area. I myself was not sure that I could finally become so close to the local people of here. Thank you for everything. You were there beside my every ups and lows. I also like you Mohan." Sneha replied in a low voice.

"But Mohan, I need a little time to think everything over. I hope you understand me."

"Sure Sneha, I can understand. I know you need time to think over my proposal and you are free to take how much time you feel like. It is finally up to you to decide whether you want to take our friendship to a next level. I also assure you, that whatever is your decision I will be always beside you. It will never hamper our current friendship." Mohan then stood up and came towards where Sneha was sitting. He then knelt beside her and took her hand into his. "I really love you Sneha. It is not some short term impulse, I myself thought over this several times in the last few days. "I was really

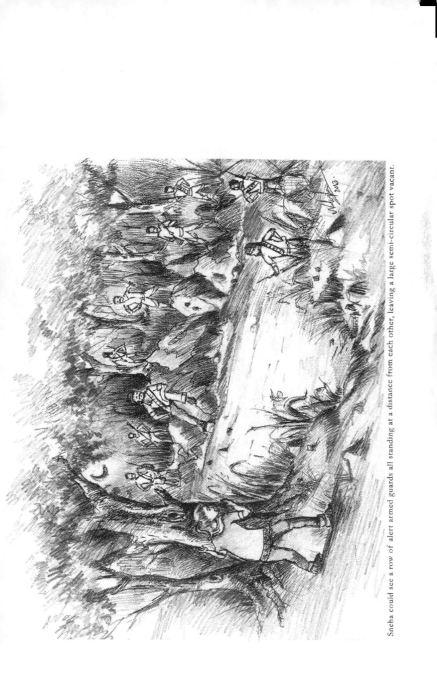

Sneha could see a row of alert armed guards all standing at a distance from each other, leaving a large semi-circular spot vacant.

worried about how you would respond ,or whether everything would be blown up. But finally I can relax and sleep in peace as I told you my feelings. Now it is up to you to take the final decision, I will never pressurise you for anything." He then lifted her hand and gave a gentle kiss on her hand.

"Good bye Sneha!"

"Good bye Mohan. Take care." Sneha replied. Mohan turned and left.

{16}

Long time after Mohan had left, Sneha kept on sitting on the veranda. She was staring towards the dark outside. She kept on thinking about the proposal of Mohan. But every time she was thinking about Mohan; Venkat was coming in her mind and clouding her thoughts. It didn't mean any sense to her. It was true that she had a crush on him, but wasn't it foolish keeping her feelings alive for him for so long. The man whom she met was so very different from her childhood crush, yet since that day she hadn't passed a single day without thinking about him. Those two pairs of intelligent eyes, how she didn't forget them even after so many years.

But after today's Mohan proposal what should be her response? She was nearing twenty four, beautiful, smart, and slim with long hair and dark eyes. It's not strange that an equally handsome Mohan would fall in love with her. She herself wanted to accept his proposal but somewhere inside her brain, the memory of her past was disturbing her.

"How silly of me?" Murmured Sneha.

She knew that most of the women of her age would surely jump into this proposal, but since her youth, she has been different. Whereas most of her friends by now were in some sort of relationship, some even had multiple boyfriends whereas some others already changed a few and wanted to explore more. She even knew a few of them even experienced physical relationship with their partners; though they didn't discuss these sorts of gossips in front her. She was the boring one, according to them, in this matter. All her friends were sure about being her single and surely unaware about her secret crush towards her brother's friend. Even her male batch mates and the junior doctors of her medical college feared her seriousness and hadn't approached her for the fear of severe rejection and reaction from her.

But that day she wanted to be happy. Officially a man finally proposed to her. The air was still for a long time. It's started raining now. The sound of raindrops filled her ears like music. The wet smell of soil filled her nostrils. She closed her eyes.

She might have slept, because she didn't know when the rain stopped. She was woken by Budhiya. She rubbed her eyes and yawned, then stretched her neck and could see Ramuna standing a little behind him. She immediately realised that she has to go in the jungle again. Budhiya was given an angry look at him.

"Say Ramuna, what I have to do again?" Sneha asked.

"Nothing serious Madam! Our Commander told me to ask you, whether you can take the pain to accompany me, once again. He wants to meet you." Ramuna replied.

"What is Venkat up to?" thought Sneha. She knew she could now easily decline to go with him and dismiss him without any fear. These Maoists would not do any harm to her. But she was curious; she had many a questions to ask Venkateswar Reddy. She made up her mind and told Ramuna that she would go.

Budhiya, whose fear of these men was also reduced, gave her a disapproving and angry grunt.

Sneha nodded towards Budhiya and told Ramuna to wait outside. She then turned towards Budhiya and said "Don't worry Budhiya. Both of us know that these people now won't do any harm to us as long as we follow their instructions. But there is also something which I want you to know." She then in a brief, told about Venkat. Told him how he and his brother were friends in their high school days. She omitted the part about her feelings towards him, but told Budhiya that there were some answers she must know.

"Don't worry, I will be all right." She told him, "Please don't tell this to anyone, I want to stay you back this time. Please don't argue with me. I know your concern towards me. But there are some answers which I should know on my own."

She then gave him a brief hug and said "You are like my guardian here. I owe you a lot. But please let me walk alone today. I will come back as early as possible."

She went inside her room and closed the door to change her dress.

{17}

The rain few hours back, really changed the interiors of the jungle. The path on which they marched a couple of times was now slippery and moist. She slipped and tripped a few times and indeed supported by Ramuna to avoid a fall. Though she always used to wear jeans and sneakers while coming to the jungles she feared today that she might come across a snake or some other similar creatures. When they were nearing the camp, she found Ramuna to make a sudden diversion and asked her to follow him. Sneha stopped and looked towards him looking for any sign of alarm. Ramuna told her that Suraj Ji was waiting at a spot not far from the camp. It was a favourite spot for him when wanted to spend a few moments for himself.

He also told her to be careful and put her feet exactly where he was putting his. These places were well guarded by land mines and one wrong step could blow both of them into pieces. When he found her dreaded expression he assured that as long as she was strictly following his steps, she had nothing to fear.

Zigzagging and carefully following Ramuna, Sneha cleared the jungle and was now standing on the bank of a small river. She could see at a distance, Venkat was sitting on a relatively large sized rock facing the river, his back facing the jungle. Glancing around, Sneha could see a row of alert armed guards all standing at a distance from each other, leaving a large semi-circular spot vacant. The large rock was roughly at the centre of the semi-circle.

Ramuna stopped and waved her to go towards the rock. She had to meet him alone. She moved towards the rock. While she was at the base of the rock, Venkat turned towards her, got down, and helped her to climb the rock. He then sat beside her. For the first few minutes both of them didn't say a word. The small river was flowing in front of them making a little rippling sound as the water hit little boulders on its course.

Both of them sat side by side for quite a long time. Then finally Shivankar spoke "Thanks Ruku for coming. I know all the risks you have to take to come here. But I know there are questions in your mind for which you seek answers. I also could not relax unless I share a few things with you. So, let me begin from the start."

"After I went to Jadavpur University, the initial few months were normal. In those months I really missed Babin, your family and especially you, Ruku!" Sneha looked towards him. Shivankar continued "Many a times, I wanted to visit your house; but somehow something had come up, every time I made a plan to visit your house. In those initial days, I kept on thinking about you. How could I forget those days, specially that afternoon when you kissed me to relieve my stress and I was so stupid to leave without saying a word to you? I even dreamt that after the completion my studies I would express my feelings to you, I was determined to prove myself, so that I should be in a better position when I would propose to you and ask your hand for marriage."

Sneha kept on staring towards the small river. Shivankar again started. "After those initial few months, something happened that changed my life forever." Sneha gave him a glance, but didn't say anything. Shivankar continued, "During my first year, I got involved in college politics and within a short period became an active member of the student union. Till then, it was ok. But when I was in the mid of my second year, I had a difference of ideology with the senior union members and found them acting against the norms of the party and sabotaging it silently. They were just discreetly working for the opposition, masking themselves as the well-wishers of the students. I threatened to expose them, but soon realised that the problem was much deeper than I anticipated, most of the senior leaders knew about that and were corrupt till the deep core of their heart. Then, my life was threatened for knowing too much."

"In that period, I was hiding, running from ex-party members, bunking classes; couldn't remember for how many days I had not returned to my hostel, slept on park benches and inside parked drainage pipes, went without bath and proper hygiene, even without food. That period was like hell to me and I was in a complete mess. Every day I was in a constant fear of death looming over my head." Shivankar closed his eyes for a second as to remember those harsh days. "Then one day a man came to me like a messiah. I initially didn't trust him and thought it was some sort of scheme of my enemies but was dumbfounded when found him to know so many things about me. We talked for a long time, about many things and surprised to find that he knew so many inside stories about my party. He asked me to accompany him to his small rented flat. I finally bathed and ate proper meal. We talked nearly for the whole night. It was he who persuaded me to return to the University."

"Then?" Sneha asked, somewhere at a distance an owl hooted as it might catch its dinner.

Shivankar resumed, "Next day, he himself accompanied me to the University. I was terrified to return but was really surprised to find that my ex-party members stared at me with burning eyes from a distance, but none dared to approach me. After again assuring me that nothing would happen to me, as by-now everybody got the message that who was behind me, he went towards the head of the department's cabin. I later came to know that he was a famous Bengali ex-Naxalite leader. I left my hostel and started living with him from that day onwards. He had become my political guru."

"Well Ruku, I don't want to drag into every detail, only that he opened a new world for me. Under his guidance I found the meaning of my life and answers to what I was seeking. He was into some secret mission, which he later revealed to me. He insisted me to complete my studies first, then if I would desire I could join him. He had a long list of followers, but I became his favourite and most obedient."

"After my studies, I, under his recommendation, joined this movement. Gone through every training required, and my dedication and hard work made me what I am today. I worked for the poorest people at Jharkhand, Orissa, Andhra Pradesh and Chhattisgarh. I am now the chief of operations in this part." Sneha sighed heavily but Shivankar seemed not to notice her and continued his narration "It's not that I had not thought about you in all these years, but my circumstances prevented me to contact you. Then something really unexpected happened. While enquiring about the new recruited doctor of the hospital, yes, we do enquire about every new entry in our areas to find out about any possible threats from the authority, I was amazed to find that it was none other than you."

"I wished to meet you but didn't know how, but destiny had different plans. And I finally met you in person on that day when you nursed me. Though, I was not in a condition to tell you anything at that time. But I was surprised when I heard about your decision to visit again, but then smiled thinking that you and only you could take such a decision. Your nature and quest to explore the unknown wasn't changed. You haven't changed. I made my mind to reveal myself. Though I was surprised that you couldn't recognise me at all, then I understood how much change I had gone through. But why you? Might be my parents couldn't recognise me."

"But why did you want to meet me or to reveal yourself in front of me last time. Because you are not the Venkat whom I knew, you had transformed completely and became Shivankar, the Maoist leader." Sneha finally replied.

"I want to meet you because I want you know about my feelings towards you. I know it doesn't matter to you, but still want to tell you that I loved you and still do. Only that, previously I was not in a position and had the courage and now we both are standing on different banks of a river. But still, I have to tell you as it was something I am carrying in my heart for a really long time. Now that I said, I am relieved of that burden."

"Why now Venkat? It's been too late." Sneha told him.

"I know Ruku. I am not expecting anything from you neither I am forcing you. I just want to explain what I felt for you and still do, and that was why I could not contact you. That's all. I know about your special friendship with ASP Singh."

Sneha kept on staring towards the small river for quite a long time. Finally she told him, "I cannot assure you of anything. I need time. Please, I want to return now. Budhiya is worrying.

"Sure Ruku." Shivankar climbed down the rock and helped her down. Seeing their meeting was over, Ramuna approached them. Before he arrived, Sneha asked Shivankar, "How can I contact you, if I want?"

"Just summon Chuniyaram and ask "How is the new calf doing?" "Shivankar replied.

Ramuna was waiting to take her back.

"Take care Ruku." Shivankar turned and shouldered his Kalashnikov which he picked up from the base of the rock.

{18}

Sneha was staring towards the human anatomical chart hanged inside her small outdoor cabin. Hardly five minutes passed since Mohan had left. Since that day, a couple of months back when he proposed to her, he regularly visited her. Though he did not bring out the topic, she could sense his mind was searching for answers. He was looking for answers in her every small gesture, but due to his extremely gentlemanliness he did not openly ask her about her reply, but she could feel how eager he was for her response.

But Sneha was in a dilemma. Why these two persons she liked, proposed to her on the very same day. She really liked Mohan, she felt safe with him, and she knew her family would also accept and like Mohan as he was such a nice person, then why she was delaying in accepting his proposal. Why, every time she Venkat came and overshadowed her mind whenever she readied herself to make a decision. She really felt guilty now days in front of Mohan.

"Guilty?"

Yes "guilty" was the perfect word.

In the past couple of months, she was leading a secret life. A life which her conscience mind didn't permit, a life she knew has no future. A life only she along with a very few others knew. A life which could land her into immense trouble and brand her working against the law, against the society, against the authority.

She still could not judge herself, why she summoned Chuniyaram that afternoon and asked him "How is the new calf doing?" It was completely out of curiosity but surprised to see Chuniyaram to nod his head at one side with folded hands and left with an expressionless face, without even staring at her.

That night Ramuna came and took her to Shivankar. She was amazed to find the network of these rebels. How discreetly they used to function. If she was not informed, she could never imagine that the chowkidar Chuniyaram was working for the Maoists. That very chowkidar who never raised his head before her, always used to appear in front of her with folded hands, she hardly heard his voice, always found him doing his duty or looking after his cows when he was not working for the hospital. That very person had been secretly working for the most wanted people of this area.

She was amazed to find that after all these years; her likeness towards Venkat was not diminished. Initially it was like inquisitiveness from her side but slowly she found herself sinking deep into it. Till now she thought herself to be a mature person, but her recent act contradicted her belief and put a question about herself in front of her own eyes.

She followed the same land mine infested path led by Ramuna, who carefully guided her. Though she was scared at the first time, slowly she gained confidence in Ramuna and now smartly followed his footsteps. She knew, she was safe as long as she didn't try anything valiant. In her last few meets she and Venkat talked about a lot of things, though most of the time Venkat was the main speaker, Sneha also joined him and asked a lot of questions to him. She found herself slowly becoming normal towards Venkat. While he told her about his vision, his belief and the reason why he chose this path, Sneha, on the other hand, was trying to visualize him about the dangers on this path. But every time she had brought up the topic, Venkat changed it.

Though till now she was unsuccessful, Sneha was determined to bring her views and put sense to him some day. But even she disagreed with his ideologies; she was surprised to find how those few years changed that shy and lean South Indian boy completely and made him a well-built man, the rebel leader named Shivankar. Like the others, he also occasionally wrapped on his head a thin traditional cotton towel, named gamchha, around his head. She always found him wearing deep olive green coloured shirts and trousers.

While Venkat talked to him, she just wanted to keep on listening to him. Whatever be the topic was, whether she agreed with him or not, she was deeply drowned into his oration. She used to forget her surroundings, and keep on listening to him the way she listened when he explained some Physics or Mathematics formula or theorem to her. She wanted to put a finger on his lips and kept on staring in his deep, intelligent eyes.

Sneha sighed heavily. She was torn between Venkat and Mohan. She liked them both. But she had to choose one among them. If she would accept Mohan's offer her life would be smooth, she knew Mohan would fulfil all her dreams and he would really do anything to keep her happy, but if she had to incline towards Venkat, all she could foresee was a doomed path lay ahead for her. She

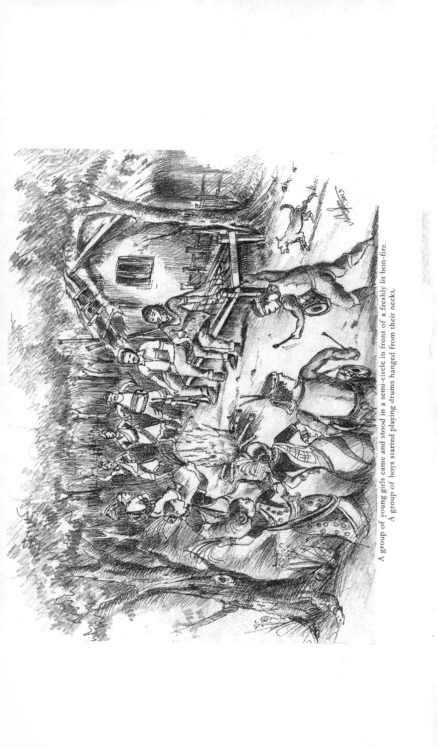

A group of young girls came and stood in a semi-circle in front of a freshly lit bon-fire. A group of boys started playing drums hanged from their necks.

could hardly imagine what would be the reaction of her family if they came to know about her recent secret ventures. She closed her eyes and again sighed heavily. Why Venkat has to come back in her life. She had nearly forgotten him. It would be so easy for her to think herself beside Mohan. But why everything turned so complicated now?

Might be she was fully responsible to make the things very complicated. Yes, she could stop herself much before. But now it's becoming too late. Every passing day she was getting more entangled in the web. She heard from her friends, that there were times when your heart rules over your brain. There were times when you fail to rationalize your acts. Previously in her college days whenever she heard these things, she laughed and told her friends that everyone had full control over what he or she did. But now she could understand what her friends meant then.

But she has to find a solution of this mess. She was thinking for the past few days about a possibility, she would bring out the topic to Venkat tonight.

"Tonight?"

Yes, tonight she was supposed to meet Venkat. Before Mohan arrived today, she summoned Chuniyaram and said the coded message. At their last meeting, Venkat promised to take her to the tribal village of Surmakee. There would be some festival in the Gond village.

The only person who knew and openly disagreed and protested to her for these night time ventures was Budhiya. He pleaded, cried and did his best to stop her but failed. He even mildly threatened to write a letter to Dr. Gupta back in Kolkata. But Sneha somehow persuaded him not to and pleaded him to give her a little time. She would do everything as before. She even assured him by saying that she was seriously thinking over ASP Mohan's proposal. Only she was visiting the camp because she knew their leader from her school days and he was a good friend of his brother.

Sneha looked towards the door when she heard footsteps of someone approaching. After a few seconds Ramuna peeked inside, partially hidden his face in a gamchha.

{19}

Sneha and Shivankar were sitting on a charpai, a traditional woven bed made of wood and rope. Shivankar kept his Kalashnikov beside him. A few of Shivankar's men were standing behind him, all of them were armed. On arrival to the village, Surmakee left them to meet her family. The village headman kept few offerings of fruits and vegetables near the feet of Shivankar. When they arrived, the villagers were hailing him by the name of Suraj Ji in their Gondi language. He introduced Sneha to the village headman, who greeted her with equal warmness. She was amazed to see how these tribal people were worshipping Shivankar.

She glanced around and found the thatched roofed mud houses of the tribe. The men wore dhotis and the women wore plain cotton saris. The women wore heavy jewellery made of silver.

Today they were celebrating a festival where young Gonds chose their marriage mates and the tribal council approved them. Sneha keenly watched the tradition for a long time. The male and female Gondi villagers sat in two different groups. One of the male rose from the group and called the name of the potential female, who then stood up and came forward. They then after a nod from the headman, asked for blessings with folded hands from the headman and his guests, in this case it's Sneha and Shivankar, and sat together in a third group. After all the couples chose each other, the headman spoke out the name of the couples and announced the closure of the event. Shivankar informed her, that they would be married off on a later auspicious date after duly consulting the stars and following astrological norms of the individuals. He also told her that if anyone had any objection to the match, they could raise their objections. But after the approval of the headman, no one could oppose to their marriage and they would be bound for life.

After that celebration, a group of young girls came and stood in a semi-circle in front of a freshly lit bon-fire. All of them were wearing similar bright orange coloured saris. Each of them flaunted heavy silver jewellery and nice traditional headdresses. A group of boys started playing drums hanged from their necks. Sneha came to know from Venkat that none of the Gond celebration would be complete without dance and music. Their rhythmic playing drums and dancing made the atmosphere intoxicated and magical and soon the newly coupled Gonds joined them. They were singing in their Gondi language, but the beat was so catchy that even Sneha, started swaying her head and clapping in rhythm. Shivankar brought his mouth near her ears and told her that the Gonds, through their dance and song, praising their legendary Queen named Durgawati, who bravely saved her kingdom from the Mughals, ultimately defeated after a ferocious battle by the third Mughal emperor.

While she and Shivankar both were enjoying the music, he took her hand into his and squeezed lightly. She looked towards him but found him looking towards the performing boys and girls. She did not try to release her hand and looked towards the fire, towards the performance. Both of them were in deep thought. Who knows what they were thinking?

Both of them lost the track of time. Only came back to the current state, when finally the music and dance stopped. They looked at each other and smiled. Shivankar released Sneha's hand. The village headman approached them and invited them to join their feast.

All of them sat in line on the ground, Sneha was beside Shivankar and Ramuna, followed by the village headman and the members of the tribal councils. The other Maoists sat on the other side, Sneha found that by this time Surmakee also joined her team. They were all served with a simple meal of rice, vegetables and meat. Shivankar told Sneha that the normal meals of these people comprised of millets and vegetables, it's only during their festivals they could afford rice and meat. After their simple but nicely cooked dinner Shivankar, Sneha, the headman and the other tribal council members sat around the bon-fire. All of them were served with a glass of Mahuaa drink. A type of liquor brewed locally from the Mahuaa flowers. Sneha knew that none of the tribal festivals would be completed without this drink. The men were discussing something in the local language which Sneha could not understand, but could feel it something serious by seeing the occasional nodding and facial expression of Shivankar.

The rest of the Maoist group now joined by Ramuna standing in a circle at a distance and having the Mahuaa drink, their mood was much lighter than this group. She found them laughing and guessed someone among them cracked some jokes. Suddenly she found herself lonely between these two groups. She accepted another glass of the drink which was offered to her by a young Gond girl.

{20}

Sneha and Shivankar quietly walking side by side, few of the Maoists were walking in front of them and a couple of them following behind. All of them were watchful and alert for any slightest movement, all of them except the two in the middle, who seemed to be lost in deep thought. It's been around fifteen minutes since this Maoist party left the Gondi tribal village. All of them were silent only their progressing boots were making crunching sounds.

After a long moment of silence Shivankar turned and said, "Ruku, do you trust me?"

Sneha was jolted from some kind of dream, she was feeling sleepy and her head had gone dizzy. It could be the individual effect of the drum beat and dance, their progress through the jungle with the constant buzz of the crickets or her two glasses of Mahuaa drink, or all in together. She replied "Uhh! Oh! Y-Yes"

"Are you all right?" asked Shivankar putting his hand across her shoulder.

"Yeah! I am fine." Replied Sneha, this time firmly.

"Fine" said Shivankar and added "Let me show you a nice place, as we were going through this part of the jungle, I am not sure when I will come again or being able to bring you here. Will you come?"

"Ok, why not." Sneha again replied.

Shivankar then told his party to stop. Ramuna came towards him and he instructed him to take the party to the camp. He would come with Sneha a little later. Ramuna seemed unsure whether he would leave their chief unprotected and insisted they should wait for him. Shivankar laughed and thanked him for his cautiousness. He then told Ramuna that he had news that none of the task force persons were anywhere near a large radius. Everyone was safe tonight. Ramuna still did not want to leave Shivankar all alone and after a little debate, it was agreed upon that Ramuna and another Maoist would wait at this place, the rest of the party would return to the camp. Shivankar would go to his desired place and come back within an hour or else they would start a search for him and Sneha.

Sneha was enjoying this conversation and was surprised to find how attached these rebels were to their leader, how strong their bonds were. All of them were like a family to each other. So many people, came from so different backgrounds, were bounded by a common objective.

Shivankar then came towards her and told; "Come"

They left the walking trail and started walking deep into the jungle. Hardly anyone put their feet in these places, everywhere there were thick branches, bushes and twigs. Sneha had to be very careful not to fall down. She silently cursed herself for having two glasses of Mahuaa liquor. Shivankar was walking steadily in her front; he was holding a knife in his hand and sometimes cutting branches, bushes and holding low lying twigs to make her pass. The full moon was giving them the necessary light. Shivankar kept on talking about how Ramuna and his other comrades protect him and how much they love him. Sneha hardly listened to him, keeping her mind cautious not to tangle herself in some twig and fell.

Finally they reached a comparatively clear place; a large lake was lying in front of her. Unlike the river bank where she met Shivankar, this place was minus the boulders and had soft grasses lain like a carpet instead. This whole place was too calm and quiet; it's like some magic spell cast over the whole place to make it such serene. The mild white moonlight filled that whole area and made this more enchanting. There was a single tree standing over this grass filled area between them and the lake. Shivankar took her towards the tree. While approaching she could smell the beautiful scent of the flowers of the tree. The tree bed is whitened by the light yellow coloured flowers. They stood below the tree and faced the lake.

"This place is so-so beautiful, so mystic, so magical. Thank you Venkat for bringing me here." Sneha could not suppress her joy.

"Thank you for liking this place Ruku. This is my most favourite spots, and I never miss a chance to visit this place whenever I am in these areas. It seems this place belongs to me, I feel so myself in this place, as if this place is made only for me." Venkat told her.

Both of them kept on looking towards the lake, enjoying the soft moonlight over its still water, holding their hands, the small yellow flowers were silently dropping on their heads, shoulders and feet. Then Venkat turned her towards him, lowered his head and kissed her. Sneha immediately responded and kissed him back, she circled his neck with her soft hands and he embraced her tightly. She felt his strong muscles allover her body. She felt one of his hands slipped and pressed her buttocks towards his body. She could feel his hardness. Sneha moaned lightly, Venkat was now kissing her cheeks, her throat.

She was waiting for this moment for so long. She was quite attractive but somehow till date these things had not happened to her. Though, in her school days she had a crush on this man, but both of them at that time were immature. But finally today she was transforming into a lady. All her resistance was tumbling down. She was slowly surrendering to him. She clutched the hair of Venkat.

Venkat then made her to lie down on the soft flowerbed; he kept on kissing her and exploring her body. It seemed to Sneha that he was also eagerly waiting for this moment. He pressed her breasts and pinched it hard. She gave out an amorous cry. She opened the buttons of his olive green shirt and touched his muscles, she stopped a while when she touched his bullet wound. He unhooked her bra and took her kurti off. She felt his lips and tongue all over her body. She found his hands fumbling over her jeans. She helped him to undress her completely. She finally felt his thrust and parted her legs. There was an initial resistance, then something broke and he was fully inside her. She uttered a rejoicing sound. The light yellow flowers kept on falling over these two bodies as if trying to bury them fully.

{21}

Sneha was lying with her head on Venkat's bare chest. He was slowly caressing and playing with her silky hair. Time seemed to have stopped for both of them. How long they had spent there; it could be ages or it could be hardly fifteen or twenty minutes. Sneha lifted her head and put her chin on his chest and looked towards him. He was looking at her with gratified eyes.

"I love you Ruku. I love you for ages. It was destiny's choice that you came here when I myself lost all hope to meet you again, but see you are here with me. If you really want something honestly, you will definitely get it."

"I love you too, Venkat." Sneha replied.

"But Venkat" she raised herself from his chest and sat beside him, "I am really worried for you. I am worried for us. What will be our future?"

Shivankar rose on his elbows and tried to say something, but Sneha continued, "I know you do live in your ideology and I don't want to agree or disagree with you. But I am sure you will definitely admit that you do live in immense danger every day. You will also admit that even I do live in danger since the day I met you and started coming to you. Do you know what will happen to me and my family if anyone comes to know about my secret life?"

She took a little pause and again started "I know both of our thinking does match at one point that both of us want to do something for the most neglected people of these areas. But do you think by taking arms and fighting against the government can really be a solution? You are fighting against a very powerful enemy, and who can say that one day they may even be able to restore peace in these areas. Then what will happen to you? To both of us? I fear for that day."

"I know that you understand the situations of these areas much better than me, as you are staying right in between them. But won't they be more help if someone from the system does something for them. I know the system is not correct. There have many a flaws in it, there are people like Sohan Lal Singh, and may be worse than him, in every stage of the system. But believe me, there are some good persons also. And I have got a chance to interact a few of them also."

Venkat stood up and walked a few steps towards the lake. His nice V-shaped torso was gleaming in bright moonlight. Sneha looked at him. He kept on staring towards the still water of the lake for a long time, as if in a deep thought. He finally spoke. "It's been too late Ruku. I myself had been dragged too deep into it, and from this position I cannot return. These poor people have their full faith in me. You just visited one village; there are several villages in these areas that see their only hope in us. They worship me as their saviour. How can I deceive them? How can I betray my own people, who are ready to give their life for me? It's not possible Ruku. Not possible for me."

Sneha stood up and walked towards him. She told him, "Since I met and came to know who you are, I was thinking about you day and night. I was thinking how to turn the clock and made you stay for me, forever and ever. I was not getting any answers, since few days back I read an article in the local newspaper. The Chief Minister of Chhattisgarh appealed to every active rebel group to lay their arms and invited them to have a peaceful talk. He asked everyone to surrender. He assured that he personally would look into the matter for ensuring minimum punishment for each individual, if they willingly surrender their arms. He will then personally look into the problems and try to solve them in a real peaceful manner. He sincerely wants peace to restore in the jungles. He also has announced a few schemes for the welfare of the poors. I am not asking you to take any drastic step, only asking you to think over the proposal. But you are free to take any decision you like."

"You are too immature to understand the politics of those people. Too immature." Shivankar replied.

"You may be right Venkat. I just ask to think over any possible solution, which can keep us together."

Shivankar didn't say anything but kept on staring towards the lake. Sneha could understand that he was in a deep thought. But could not understand what he was thinking. She moved a little close to him and embraced him from his right side and put her head into his chest and filled her nostrils with his scent. Both of them were bathing in the gleam of moonlight. They stood like this for quite a long time, suddenly an owl flew over their heads and flew deep into the forest.

"Let's move Ruku. Ramuna would be very worried if we don't return in time."

They started returning. Sneha glanced for a last time to this heavenly place. This place would always be special to her. She hoped to return here soon, though not sure when she would again get a chance to visit, might be some other full moon night. She secretly named this place her "Garden of Eden". She turned and found Shivankar waiting for him.

Both of them didn't say anything while they returned. She again carefully followed Shivankar. Finally they reached the spot where Ramuna and the other Maoist were waiting.

Seeing them coming back, Ramuna came towards them, "You are fifteen minutes late. If you didn't turn up in the next five minutes, we were planning to go on a search for you two."

"Sorry Ramuna for keeping you waiting and worrying you." Shivankar told him. "Let's go."

Four of them started walking towards the place where they had to leave their jeep for visiting the Gondi village.

While returning, Sneha fell into deep asleep. She was woken by Ramuna only after returning near Gongapal General Hospital. She was found the jeep was empty except the driver, Ramuna and herself. She cursed herself for falling asleep, as she didn't get a chance to say goodbye to Venkat. She had no idea when he and the other Maoist got down.

{22}

Budhiya came and informed that ASP Singh had arrived and he sat in the drawing room. The month of October had arrived. Though in the daytime it was still warm, the nights in this area were slowly turning cold. A few days had passed since her return from the tribal village. She kept on thinking about the time spent with Venkat. She was thinking about how to be together with Venkat for ever. She thought about many possibilities but dismissed all one by one. Finally she thought about one person who could help her, whom she could trust.

That person only could show her some path. She knew the time had come for her to confess before him and to tell him the truth. She called up Mohan in the morning and asked him if he could manage to come to her this evening. Mohan initially was taken aback because she never asked him to visit. It's he who arranged their meeting. After assuring him everything was fine, Mohan promised her that he would come in the evening.

Sneha wrapped the light shawl over her housecoat and came to the drawing room. He found Mohan turning the pages of a magazine. Seeing her, he put it down and greeted her. Sneha thanked her for coming. Budhiya placed two cups of hot tea on the small table.

For a few moments both of them sat quietly, sipping tea from their respective cups. Sneha was preparing herself for what she was going to say to Mohan. Though she rehearsed what and how much she would tell him, but now in front of Mohan she was all jumbled up.

Finally she cleared her throat, put down her cup and began; "Thank you Mohan for coming. I know you are a busy man and it's really been difficult for you to arrange in such a short time. All our previous meetings were much pre-planned as you arrange it according to your and my schedule. But today I am really sorry to ask you to come like this on such a short notice. I need your help desperately. Please help me." She pleaded the last line.

Mohan put his hand on hers and pressed "No need to worry. Just tell me what happened. I will do my best and go to my extreme to help you. Just tell me what happened."

"Thank you!" Sneha replied.

"But before I tell you anything, let me tell you one thing that after I came here, you have become my true friend, my best friend. I trust you completely. I really appreciate your proposal and your concern towards me. But I need to tell you something. I am sure you will understand my dilemma after hearing my full story; you can understand why I didn't say yes to your proposal till date. But please don't take me wrong; let me finish the whole story. Please don't interrupt me in between. You will understand everything at the end." Sneha took a small pause.

Mohan was surprised, but didn't say anything.

Then slowly Sneha told him everything. How she was abducted, how she nursed the Maoist. Why she had visited the camp for the second time and came to know who their leader was. How she came to know about the leader of the Maoists, was none other than the boy whom she knew quite well from her yesteryears. She even told him that how coincidentally on the same day both he and the Maoist leader proposed to her. She told him about her girlish crush on her brother's friend who turned out to be the Maoist leader. She told him about her secret night-time visits to the leader. She even told her about her last visit to the tribal village of the Gonds. The only part of the story she omitted was her visit to her secret "Garden of Eden." She also did not mention Chuniyaram's role in all this.

Sneha noticed how Mohan's facial expression kept on changing. First surprised, then anger, then awe and finally expressionless the way he was sitting now.

Mohan kept on sitting like this for a long time, occupied in deep thought. Finally said; "What have you done? You are in a complete mess. It is very difficult to take you out of this."

Sneha lowered her face and said; "I know; but it was not me for whom I called you to come today. I need a suggestion from you. Is there any way to take Venkat out of this situation? Suppose if he surrenders, can your authority be merciful and show sympathy towards him? Or if you can capture him and his team alive, can your authority be lenient towards him, if he is ready to co-operate with the authority?"

"Right now, I can't assure you anything. Because you are not asking me to deal with some petty criminal, but the most notorious Maoist in this area if not one of the most sought after Maoist in this country, and if he surrenders the decisions regarding him will come, not from me but from much higher positions from my reach". He paused, "But, yes if he surrenders or co-operates after being captured, I am sure that he will be given a chance to reform. But the way he is living now sooner or later he will meet the destiny which both of us know. But let's not think about it now."

"Tell me whatever you know, everything you know about these camps and its surroundings. Let me see, what best I can do. But let me assure you, whatever you say is completely out of the book, nothing will be recorded. It's entirely between you and me. I am assuring you nothing will happen to you."

Sneha told him whatever she knew. How she visited the camp and later the mine packed river bank. While she was telling this, she thought whether she was making a mistake. By doing this, was she completely breaking the trust of the person she loved the most or she was helping Venkat to return to the normal life. She prayed to God that her worries to be proved wrong. She dearly loved

Venkat and Mohan was her only hope to help her out. She prayed to God for the safety of both of these men.

After Sneha completed her narration, both of them sat quietly for a long time. Finally Mohan rose and walked towards the door. He turned and told her, "Ok! Let me see what I can do. I will never let any harm happen to you."

He turned and left. The clock ticked to fifteen minutes past eight.

Sneha sighed heavily and closed the door. She was in deep thought whether she had committed the biggest mistake of her life. The mistake for which she would have to regret for her entire life. But what options did she have? Why her life had to be so complicated?

Her eyes became moist. She started weeping. Budhiya came and stood with a glass of water.

{23}

There was severe banging at her door. Sneha was jerked from her sleep. Someone was continually knocking at her door, she hurriedly left the bed and opened the door of her bedroom. Budhiya was standing with a horrified face. He informed her there was an emergency at the hospital. She was required there as soon as possible. Sneha had no time to think. She asked Budhiya to give her five minutes.

What could this be? Her heart sank, she was sure this was some bad news. A week had passed since her conversation with Mohan and every passing day she feared for some bad news. Though initially she hoped for some good news, but with every passing day her hope diminished. She quickly changed and came outside to find Budhiya was also ready to accompany her.

She rushed towards the hospital building. The middle aged Budhiya tried his best to keep in pace with her, but Sneha was running for life. By now she could sense what had happened. On reaching the steps, she found the place was filled with task force constables. Inside the corridor she found a row of bodies lying. Few of them were crying in pain but most of them were already silent. She was shocked to recognise their faces. Surmakee was lying as if in deep sleep. Sneha found a glimpse of a smile on the lips. She also found the blood stained face of Ulupi. A fighter like Ulupi who had faced so many tortures in her life finally could find the eternal peace. She moved forward. The wounded were already attending by the hospital staffs.

She found a figure lying on a stretcher and rushed towards it. She shouted loudly when she found it was none other than Ramuna. A constable was standing beside him. He was also crying, but his condition was better than many. On examining she found, he had a bullet wound on his left thigh, but the bullet grazed him. She pushed him a dose of morphine to ease his pain. Soon he would sleep. Before he passed out, he told Sneha that it was like any other day at the camp, but suddenly without any warning firing started from everywhere. They were caught off guard but recovered quickly and fired back. But anyhow, the task force was better informed tonight. It seems that they knew their exact location and sealed their every possible escape route, he never saw the task forces so well prepared like they have the complete map of the area. They attacked from three sides leaving the mine filled river side open. When few of them took that route, they found the river was also covered by police boats. No one could escape tonight, either killed or captured. He last saw Suraj Ji fighting fiercely, but then in the utter disorder and confusion, he lost him. It seemed to him that someone betrayed them. Ramuna finally told her before passing.

Sneha checked his pulse and found it feeble but stable. She instructed the attendant to look after him. She was searching Venkat, but could not find him anywhere. She then moved towards the operation theatre and found its door open. She approached the door and saw Mohan standing inside. His head was lowered. He was holding his service cap in his hands. Sneha looked to his right and saw a body lying on a table fully covered head to toe in a white sheet. She knew who was lying below the white sheet. She closed her eyes, tears filled her cheeks.

She moved towards Mohan and before he could say anything, she slapped him hard and without thinking or saying anything, she slapped him again. Mohan did not protest. She then clenched her fist and banged on his broad chest and cried.

"Why? Why Mohan? Why?"

"I trusted you." She suddenly found she could not stand any longer, as if she lost all control on her knees and slumped on the floor. She covered her face and continued shedding tears. Mohan knelt beside her.

"I know I have betrayed you. But please listen to me." Mohan pleaded her. Sneha did not stop crying. Mohan told her, "When I returned from your bungalow, initially I was thinking how to handle the situation peacefully. I kept awake for the whole night, but could not find any answer. But I don't know when it happened but I found my emotions slowly turning into anger and finally it turned to jealousy. Yes, I was jealous to your Venkat. I loved you so dearly but you lost your heart to someone like him. For the next few days, anger and jealousy had completely taken over my mind, I was so under it that I completely forgot about your plea and request. I was like under some kind of spell, I completely lost my sense when I made my plan to attack the camp and briefed my team."

"I completely followed your description while I made the plan to attack the camp, and completely covered it from all sides. But when the attack started, and I saw the first Maoist to fell, my senses came back to me. But till then, it was too late. The arrow had left the bow. They fought fiercely and bravely but by then I was trying to locate their leader, your Venkat, to capture him alive, so that at least I can keep your word. But I was too late."

"I heard about a severe resistance from the left side of the camp and sensed that Venkat could be there. I tried my best to reach him fast, but when reached there, I found the firing stopped. I rushed there without caring for my life, but found three dead Maoists and a heavily injured man. It's none other than your Venkat. He was still alive; I told him your name and surprised to find that he immediately recognised me and called me by my name. I arranged a jeep to carry him to the hospital and sat beside him. He was holding my hand and both of us talked a little. Though he was in severe pain, he didn't let me stop him. Before we reached the hospital, he realised that I also loved you and I realised what a disastrous mistake I had done. But as we entered the hospital gate, he passed holding my hands on my lap. Before he died, he gave me this to give you."

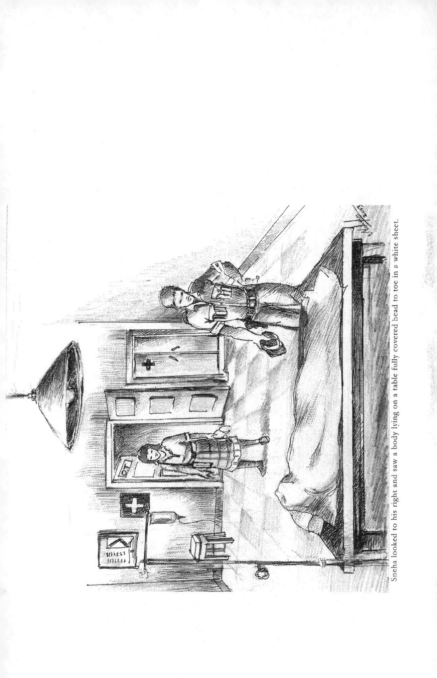

Sneha looked to his right and saw a body lying on a table fully covered head to toe in a white sheet.

Looking towards his outstretched hand, Sneha saw a German silver chain with a small locket, she recognised it immediately. Many a summers back, it was the smallest gift, the only gift presented to him by Sneha on his birthday just a few months before their exams. She was surprised to find it was still treasured by Venkat. Well it was, because the man who treasured it, now lying dead on the cold table in this very room.

"I am extremely sorry, Sneha." Mohan again started. "The mistake I had done was very severe. But please believe me, I love you deeply. Whatever I had done is only to win your love back. I became completely blind in jealousy."

Sneha stopped him. "No need to say sorry. Because saying sorry cannot bring that dead man alive. I don't want to judge your act. You had done whatever you thought was correct. But, I do want to suggest you something. You are a nice person. You have a bright future ahead. You will definitely win Governor or President's medal. But please don't break anyone's trust in the future. I completely trusted you and that was why I gave you every detail. If anyone was responsible for so many deaths, it's no one but me. And it's me who has to carry this pain till my end."

"You will definitely get a perfect match for you in future. But next time don't break her faith. I will remember you as a good friend. But please never try to contact me ever or try to come in front of me. Because whenever I will see you, you will remind me of this pain. You will remind me that you killed the person I had loved. You have lost me. Good luck for your future." Sneha wiped her tears and took the locket from his hand. She then stood up and went outside the operation theatre.

Mohan kept on kneeling down.

{24}

On the next morning, she did not leave her room. She did not come out when Budhiya asked her to have lunch. By late afternoon she opened her door and came out. She assured Budhiya that she was all right. She then called up her Papa and had a long talk. She told him that she wanted to come back. She did not tell him what happened but he could sense from that distance there was something wrong. Though he did not pressurise her by asking what had happened. He would have enough time for it after she would return.

She then had a long talk with her mother. After she hung-up, she told Budhiya to make her simple dinner.

After dinner, she again retarded to her room. All the events since her arrival kept on playing in front of her eyes. She had visualised the same things several times today. She had fallen in love with this place, with the simple people of this place. But after what had happened last night, she could not stay here any longer. The whole place was too much filled with the memories of the two persons he liked the most. She lost both of them.

As the night progressed, she finally decided that she had no other option but to resign. She had failed in her mission. She came here to work for the poor whom she was doing sincerely, but in the middle somehow she was entrapped between the two, who were a complete contrast to each other. If she could control herself at the right time, then she didn't have to face this day.

Finally she started typing her resignation letter. She deleted and retyped it several times. She finally agreed on the draft and took the print out. She put the letter inside a white envelope and wrote the name of the Honourable Health Minister above it.

She would submit the letter in the morning.

By 6AM, she came and sat on the veranda. Budhiya placed a hot cup of tea in front of her on the small cane table.

She looked in front of her. Her eyes were again turning moist. Some unknown bird kept on chirping at a distance. The sound of it again made her sad; she wiped her eyes with the corner of her shawl.

*   *   *

. . . Deepak completed his narration, both Subhashis and Anuraddha staring at him. They couldn't believe what they just heard. Slowly both of them lowered their eyes; Deepak guessed he had seen tears in Anuraddha's eyes.

The rain outside seemed to ease a bit, though it was not stopped.

Deepak again started in a low voice, "Last when I heard this story, I didn't understand the slight emotional parts. I came back and thought about it, initially I thought how foolish Ruku di was, then thought Mohan was right to eliminate one of the enemies of the state, then again thought that Mohan had no right to interfere into the matter of Ruku di and Venkat as Ruku di never accepted his proposal, I then thought Mohan had betrayed by taking advantage of the simplicity of my cousin sister. I was totally confused that night and the next couple of days. Then I slowly started realising the full aspect of the events happened to my cousin sister." He paused "All three of them were correct in their respective places. While Ruku di's plan was to reform Venkat and save his life, Venkat was committed to his ideology though according to us it was wrong, he was loyal to it, on the other hand Mohan was also committed to his work, his duty and responsibility. The connections between those were really very complicated."

"Initially I thought why Ruku di left everything and came back. She could ignore Mohan and do her duty, when she choose to go there for a noble cause despite the opposition of her family, I felt really proud of her. That's why I was shocked when I heard her return, leaving her mission half way. But after I heard the Mariam's story and your discussion, I realised why she fled from the place full of memories of her close ones. But before taking any action couldn't Mohan discuss the matter with Ruku di?"

"I can answer your query." Subhashis said. "Look Deep, according to our ancient books our life is surrounded by six passions who are also our enemies. They are lust, anger, avarice, blind attachment, vanity and jealousy. These passions or ripus should not be kerbed; they should be expressed and practised in a measured way or else they will find out their way through another or more than one passion." Sensing both Deepak and Anuraddha giving him an inquisitive look, he keeps on elaborating it "As in this case, Mohan was in love with Ruku di, but he was kept waiting for a long time, so when he heard that the person he liked, was in love with a different person, that too one of his enemies, he couldnot supress his anger and jealousy.

Especially when the sixth passion named jealousy engulfs your mind, you will fail to realise the mistakes you are doing under its spell. Ultimately we all are driven by our emotions, hope I can make my view understandable."

Both Deepak and Anuraddha nodded their heads in appreciation.

After a brief moment's silence Anuraddha spoke; "Well friends, we three had got enough food to nourish our individual brains for the coming week. I think now we should call it a day. The rain is continuing and if we stay late it would be very difficult to get transportation."

"Hmm!! Yes!!" Subhashis said and stretched himself on the chair. "This evening was really going fine, we can continue for hours. But ultimately we all have to leave."

Deepak also stretched himself. The idea of again stepping outside in this rain really irritated him. Why the rain didn't stop while they were inside for so long.

"How will you two return?" Deepak asked his friends.

"I will catch the Metro as always. It is the most convenient mode for me, and seeing this weather I am even confident to get a seat inside also." Subhashis replied. Both of his friends laughed on hearing this. Every time Subhashis complained that he never gets a seat at Metro railway. Subhasish stays near Sobhabazar, at northern part of the city. "And you too?"

"I will catch a cab. I really hate moving in a public transport in this weather, that too in this late evening. The buses will crawl at their own wish and speed; in this weather they know that there will be fewer passengers but still they will wait unnecessarily and let the few boarded passengers at their mercy. So cab would be best for me. I will really appreciate when the Metro completes its extension to our area. I will drop Anuraddha on my way." Deepak answered.

"Its fine Deepak, I can manage. I stay just a few stoppages from Park Street; it will be fine for me." Anuraddha mildly opposed.

"It's completely out of question Anu. We cannot leave you alone, no matter how much independent you are." Both Deepak and Subhashis objected strongly.

Subhasis added "Both of you stayed at South Kolkata. As Deep stayed at Garia and your home at Hazra falls in his route, he will drop you and then go. We cannot leave you alone at night, especially in this rainy weather."

"Ok! As you two wish. But Subha, we will share the fare." She smiled and said. She then called the waiter for their bill.

After the payment with a fair amount of tip, time had come for the three friends to say good-bye to each other. They hugged each other and readied to leave the tea bar. "Why don't you come with us, we will drop you at the gate of Park Street Metro station. No need to walk till the station in rain." Deepak told his friend.

They waved the staff of the tea bar, promised to come next week and left.

The three legged tea table on which they were seated for so long was left with three empty cups. Soon a waiter came and cleared it. Those three were the last customers to leave. In this weather there was hardly any chance for any new customer to come. The people outside were heading towards the different kind of watering holes.

The clock above the door showed 8:45PM.

The incessant rain outside was continuing with the boring pitter-patter, though it seemed to weaken a little bit more. May be, by the beginning of the new week the depression will be cleared.

One of the staffs of the tea bar came near the door and turned the sign to CLOSED.

THE END